Wayward

The Bakazi Series

K.C. Harris

Owl Write Publishing

Copyright © [2024] by [K.C. Harris]

All rights reserved.

No portion of this book may be reproduced in any form without written permission from the publisher or author, except as permitted by U.S. copyright law.

Dedication

To my readers, thank you for giving my story a chance. I hope it makes you smile.

A special thanks to my special guys. I would have never completed this book without your encouragement.

Contents

Glossary	VII
Wayward	IX
1. Prologue	1
2. Chapter One	6
3. Chapter Two	19
4. Chapter Three	28
5. Chapter Four	36
6. Chapter Five	49
7. Chapter Six	55
8. Chapter Seven	62
9. Chapter Eight	69
10. Chapter Nine	79

11.	Chapter Ten	88
12.	Chapter Eleven	93
13.	Chapter Twelve	104
14.	Chapter Thirteen	114
15.	Chapter Fourteen	123
16.	Chapter Fifteen	133
17.	Chapter Sixteen	144
18.	Chapter Seventeen	158
19.	Chapter Eighteen	163
20.	Chapter Nineteen	169
21.	Chapter Twenty	177
22.	Epilogue	186
23.	The End	188
24.	Content Warning	189

Glossary

bakazi - (n.) Supernatural beings who originated on the continent of Africa. These beings have magic powers over the elements to protect and enhance nature. Sometimes called bakazi fae.

blue stone - (n.) A rare quartz stone that protects the bakazi and enhances their magic. Also known as llanite. This stone can only be found in the Texas Hill Country.

enforcer - (n.) A saam mercenary who is primarily paid to collect on demon deals and contracts. They are an unexplainable and rebellious mutation who think for themselves and refuse any orders that do not benefit them. Born with no pigment in hair strands. Can be born with or without the loss of pigment around the eyes typical of saam.

kin squad - (n.) Group of spawn sworn to protect and serve the royal family. As such they are tasked with enforcing bakazi law and investigating possible lawbreakers within the bakazi community by the royal family.

kipeyo - (n.) An insect with two pairs of large, delicate, and usually colorful wings.

pull - (n) Magnetic attraction between two magical beings, usually bakazi, who are destined to bond together in a relationship.

saam - (n.) Offspring of a zakari and a human. Used as foot soldiers to carry out the plans of their sires. Characterized by areas with loss of pigment around the eyes and loss of pigment in hair strands.

seeker - (n.) Bakazi who can see the future.

siliana - (n.) Bakazi who can project thoughts, hear others' thoughts, and sometimes control them.

silver - (n.) Mercury. Usually given as an injection. This is the only way to strip a bakazi's powers permanently. Used as punishment for breaking certain laws.

spawn - (n.) Offspring of saam or zakari and bakazi.

tari - (n.) Bakazi who have the power to heal.

wayward - (n.) Bakazi who walked away from or have no knowledge of their magical heritage.

zakari - (n.) High-level demon identified by white facial markings similar to a tattoo. Enemies of the bakazi.

Wayward

Prologue

Thirty-Two Years Ago

Meadow's throat burned. Her ears rang so much she could no longer hear her own screams. Maybe her voice had given out or maybe she had just stopped screaming and given up. No one was coming to her rescue.

Her blue stone bracelet lay useless in her backyard where the assault began. The talisman was sliced off her wrist. Defensive cuts burned along her hands and arms. Her attacker didn't use his magic. He was enjoying the fight.

Meadow tried to control her breathing. Some of her blond curls escaped her ponytail and clung to her sweat-dampened skin. She watched the four-inch blade and braced for the next attack. The zakari smiled before lunging at her again. Black mist appeared in front of her this time and the demon disappeared. A second later he wrapped his thick arms around her waist and throat from behind. She struggled against the hold, but he was too strong. Her only hope of escape would be to scatter her cells and fly but she could not calm herself enough to use any of her gifts. It was a losing battle. She would die tonight.

The zakari bent his head to Meadow's neck and inhaled loudly. His large hand gripped her belly as he drew another deep breath, pulling in her scent.

"Mmm. You are ripe, little bakazi and I like your fire. Come on, fight me some more. I like to work for my meal."

The foul smell of vanilla and ashes assaulted her senses with his every word. His face was so close that she had no trouble seeing the intricate lines of his white facial markings, even against his pale skin.

"Let me go!" she said, trying once more to pull away.

"Oh no, little bakazi. You will be my favorite new pet. You will produce fierce offspring and I will enjoy planting my seed inside you. I've always liked the smell of yellow-haired bitches."

One rough hand closed around her breast, sparking the fight in her.

"No. Help! Help me! Somebody help me!"

The zakari laughed, showing his sharp teeth and enjoying her panic.

"Meadow!" a familiar voice shouted from outside the house.

A moment later her front door swung open with a crash. Her future husband stood in the ruined doorway. He was brave but no match for a zakari demon. Not by himself.

"Rye! It's a zakari! Go get help!" Meadow yelled praying her mate would not be too stubborn to listen to her warning.

A moment later Rye rushed into the room. His brown eyes round as he took in the horror of her assault.

"Shit! Let her go!" Rye commanded, clenching his fists at his sides.

To her surprise, the thing complied. It released its hold so suddenly that Meadow stumbled backward, losing her footing.

Neither of them saw the black mist that formed behind Rye.

"Meadow, come on let's get out—"

Rye's words were cut short by the demon's thick arm around his throat.

"She's mine," said the zakari before slicing the blade across Rye's throat and letting him fall to the floor.

"Rye! No!" Meadow crawled over to the person she was supposed to marry. Blood. There was so much blood. His frantic eyes searched her face before becoming a blank stare. He was gone.

"Murdering your lover makes my dick hard and your screams are the cherry on top. You will stay in Madalie with me and birth many warriors for the zakari, but you are mine. I will not share your fight with another."

Meadow burst to her feet and charged at the demon. Her fists pounded against his chest and shoulders, pushing him to fight back and begging him to end her life.

"Kill me!" she implored.

A deep ominous chuckle escaped the demon's throat as he bear-hugged Meadow against his body, effectively ending her attack. He smoothed a finger along her cheek, gathering her tears. The world was starting to go white. Either she was about to faint, or it was the beginning of a premonition.

"Such extraordinary blue eyes. I like seeing the wetness in them. Like two overflowing pools on your stubborn face."

Then the demon's voice floated away, and she could hear a stern female voice.

Meadow could see herself lying on a bed. The voice was coming from the dark-haired young lady next to her. This was her future.

"You can do it," said the dark-haired beauty.

"I can't," future Meadow replied.

"You can. One more push and we get to meet little Jack. The twins are kicking up a storm to welcome their friend. Can't you just imagine little Jack with Wynter, and Carver building sandcastles on the beach together?" the woman said while rubbing her own swollen belly.

"The beaches of Madalie will make a wonderful playground for our spawn," said a deep voice.

Both women's bodies stiffened at the new arrival. It was her attacker. The zakari had been true to his word.

"Please, don't take him from me. Please let me care for him."

"I still love the look of tears in your eyes," he smiled. His sharp fangs were on full display. "You will care for him until he is old enough for combat training."

Future Meadow's head nodded, and she let out a guttural scream. A moment later the sharp cry of a new set of lungs filled the room.

Meadow held her breath, waiting to see the face of her future son. She could see a full head of blond hair and then the world started to go white again. The baby's cries were fading. The vision was falling apart. She was left staring into the cruel face that belonged to the father of her future child, and he was smirking down at her.

"If you survive the birth of our sons and I find another as tasty as you, I will grant this request for death, little bakazi."

Chapter One

Falling to her death is not the way Autumn thought her life would end. But here she was falling face first to the earth with no parachute. As she got closer to her final resting place, she started to recognize the scene below. The thick oak and cedar trees and a crescent-shaped rock formation signaled a familiar place. She was crashing toward the Llano River, and it was glowing. Bright blue twinkling lights lined the ground on either side. They looked like cobalt stars that had fallen to earth. Autumn felt as if gravity was not the only force drawing her to the river or the blue ground stars. She wanted to see them up close. She wanted to touch those stars and as crazy as it seemed, she knew they wanted to be touched by her. So maybe they wouldn't take her life in the process. If only she had some way to slow her downward progress.

The next second, Autumn realized her swift plunge had slowed as if she commanded it.

CHAPTER ONE

She floated like a dandelion on the breeze until she ended up hovering over the water. None of this made sense. She was face down over the river like Super Girl mid-flight wondering how to make it to dry land when she noticed something was there moving just below the surface. Make that someone.

The details of the person's face were hard to see through the water. Long dark hair floated around like a graceful shadow as she looked all around. At least Autumn assumed the person was female from what she could see. The woman's outstretched arms frantically searched for something. A way out? The woman paused as she noticed Autumn hovering above the surface. She stopped struggling to stare at Autumn through the murky water as if seeing a long-lost friend. A hand stretched out and Autumn realized the mysterious woman was reaching for her.

As terrified as she was, it would be cruel to leave the woman to a watery grave. Autumn slowly stretched her arm out toward the woman. She had been uneasy around the water since she was a child. She had a fleeting thought that the woman might pull her under but that was fear talking. Scary unwelcome memories. Doing the right thing was scary sometimes. The cloudy water started to clear just as her fingertips broke the surface. Then as if an alarm had been tripped, a loud beeping started.

Autumn gasped and coughed as she sat up. She was in her bed. In her room. Safe. The digital clock on her nightstand read 8:16AM.

KNOCK! KNOCK! KNOCK!

"Are you up?" said a familiar voice from the opposite side of Autumn's closed bedroom door.

"Uh... um yeah, Kam. I'll be out in a minute," Autumn replied while grasping the gold ring that hung on the silver chain around her neck. Something she often did when she was scared or uneasy. And these weird dreams always left a knot in her stomach. It was the fourth one in two weeks and they were getting more unsettling.

"Are you okay?" Kam asked.

Autumn took a deep calming breath before replying. Kamara could always tell when something was bothering her, and Autumn wasn't ready to share the details of her crazy dreams yet. Not even with her best friend. They didn't mean anything anyway. Bad dreams were perfectly normal, and she didn't want to worry Kam with her stupid dreams.

"I'm fine, Kam. Not everyone can be like you in the mornings, Ms. Sunshine."

"Fine." Kamara laughed. "But muffins are fresh out of the oven, and I need a taste tester."

Just the motivation Autumn needed to get moving.

"Mmmm. Okay but give me a few minutes to get ready for work first. I'm like 80 percent sure Allen is gonna fire me if I'm late again."

"He is not gonna fire you. Those kids adore you."

"And I adore them which is why I don't want to get fired," Autumn responded, opening her bedroom door to head for their shared bathroom.

CHAPTER ONE

Twenty minutes later Autumn sat across the table from her best friend. The house they shared was small, but it did include a breakfast nook with a bay window overlooking the front yard.

"So, what do you think?" Kamara asked. "More cranberries or less cranberries?"

"It's perfect. I think these are my new favorite muffins."

"You say that about all my food."

"Well, I mean it every time. You're a genius in the kitchen. Your food speaks to my soul. The Waffle Shack does not deserve you," Autumn said, absently rubbing the back of her neck.

"How's your head?" Kam asked.

Why did she always have to be so observant?

"Oh, much better," Autumn replied in what she hoped was a convincing tone.

Autumn overheated about two weeks ago while pulling some weeds and passed out in the front yard. Thankfully Kamara left work early that day and found her near the front steps. Too much longer in the sun and she might have had a heat stroke. When Autumn woke up, someone was playing a cymbal inside her head and shining a police searchlight in her eyes. At least if felt that way. Probably a concussion. The ground was hard in central Texas. There were quartz veins all over the place and she had surely hit her head when she fell.

Kam insisted on taking her to the hospital but that was a no-go. A hospital room was where she'd learned about her mom's death. She did not want to navigate those feelings again. Instead, Kamara made a terrible herbal remedy for her. It smelled like sweaty onions and old potatoes, but it did the trick. Autumn felt great. The only lingering effects seemed to be these strange dreams and ringing in her ears, but she didn't dare mention either to Kam for fear of another herbal fix.

"I better get going," Autumn said, grabbing a muffin for the road and tossing her empty cup in the sink.

"Don't forget about Lavender tonight, Autumn."

But Autumn was already out the door and pretended not to hear the invitation. She was not the night owl Kam was, and she really didn't want to get all dressed up to go to the club.

She took another bite of her muffin, hopped in her blue Honda hatchback, and headed off to work. The homemade breakfast confection perfumed the cabin. The smell of oranges always made her happy, but anything that Kamara cooked had that effect. Her roommate was magic in the kitchen.

"She's a fucking whore!" shouted Jack's current punching bag.

The loud popping sound of a bone breaking made Jack smile, but Clay's screeching hurt his ears.

It was crazy that such a high pitch could come from such a large man. Well, not exactly a *man*. Clay was a six foot, two hundred and eighty plus pound piece of elephant shit who liked to beat his family. Clay's younger sister, Ivy, asked for a meeting with the kin squad. When she arrived, she had a broken hand and a black eye. Her brother punched her in the face because she got home late from a party. Which is why he was sitting on a bucket at a rock quarry at the ass crack of dawn.

"Staying out late does not make her a whore. You broke her hand so she couldn't touch any men. I broke your arm so you can't beat any women."

Jack got right in Clay's now red face.

"Ivy is moving out. Sage is helping her pack her things right now."

"She can't do that! Ivy is the only family I have. I love her."

Jack's vision went bright blue. He was losing his grip on his emotions.

The fact that this bastard was allowed to have a family stoked the fire in Jack's chest. No one was afraid of Clay passing along his violent DNA to the next generation. "That's right, she *is* your family, and you don't deserve her. I should slit your fucking throat right now." Jack ran his hand through his long mohawk before turning his back on his prey. "But that's not what Queen Rayvn wants," he continued.

"Please, just let me apologize to my sister."

"You will stay away from your sister. You know the law. This was your warning. If you touch her again you get the silver."

"No! Please. I'm sorry. You have to tell Ivy I'm sorry. I won't touch her. I won't touch her."

The reaction was always the same whenever he mentioned the silver. Mercury injection. It was the only thing that could strip a bakazi's powers permanently.

"Please, man. You can trust me. Please. I won't—"

"Enough," Jack groaned before landing a jab to Clay's face. This asshole needed to take a little nap.

Aww. The beautiful sounds of unconsciousness.

Jack closed his eyes to savor the quiet. Though the members of the kin squad rarely worked without a partner, Jack decided to handle this alone. He knew it would be light work and it would give him time to think. He had to protect the bakazi people.

Most of the lore labeled the bakazi as faeries but most of the lore was wrong. Some bakazi would tag on the word fae. Jack thought they used the word like a default setting. Kinda like saying you need to Google something even when you're browsing with Bing or Yahoo. His people may have some of the same powers as the fae but they were not the same beings. They didn't live under toadstools or fly around on delicate wings. And they weren't all goodness and light, especially those like Jack.

The bakazi in him was strong and sure but that was only half. Jack fought the temptations of the other part of his DNA for years but in the past couple weeks, something changed. That other part of him was trying to claw and chew its way out and no matter what Jack did he knew a change was inevitable.

Something was coming. He needed time alone to think of a way to handle this. Just peace and quiet.

"Jack."

Well, there goes my quiet, Jack thought.

"I don't need a partner on this or a babysitter, Carver. I'm finished anyway," Jack said walking in the opposite direction.

"I know you asked for space, but the queen has requested an audience," Carver replied.

That was the one thing guaranteed to stop Jack's forward momentum.

"When?" Jack asked.

"Now."

"All right," Jack said, sparing a glance at Carver. "Has the squad been informed?"

"No," said Carver. "You don't understand. The queen requested a private audience with *you.*"

"Shit," Jack said through clenched teeth.

And there went his peace.

The queen had asked for a private meeting with him. Had she learned about his problem? Did she know how close the darkness within him was to the surface? He had been restless. The constant battle in his mind made it hard to sleep. With sleep came the unbearable nightmares.

Jack and Carver flew back to Base. Scattering their cells and transporting themselves in a camouflage of atmospheric haze got them to their destination a lot faster than a one-two march. It was a smart choice when the queen was waiting, and Jack was surely not going to walk into the mansion in his blood-splattered clothes. He needed time to shower and change.

The mansion stood on the north lawn. It had been built many years ago to house the rulers of the race when they left the continent. The three-story brick structure was updated within the last ten years. It went from classic colonial to modern farmhouse. Other single-family homes were built on the acreage over the years serving as a homestead for peaceful bakazi.

On the south lawn just behind a grove of trees, stood a two-story barn-dominium the kin squad referred to as Base. The kin squad was a group of males and Sage who protected their race. A race that was not as close-knit as it used to be. Some bakazi were not even aware of their magical heritage now. Others harbored a grudge over some unfulfilled ancient bullshit prophecy. The kin squad was well aware of their heritage. Unfortunately, you could not choose your genetic lineage and the bloodlines of the entire squad were...tainted.

After a quick shower, Jack headed to meet with Queen Rayvn. Jack walked over the brown and blue speckled tile of the entryway and headed for the first-floor office. The queen was waiting in an oversized chair near a window. The long casual dress she wore hid any trace of the form beneath. Feet tucked up underneath herself fidgeting with the rings on her hands, she managed to make herself look even smaller than her already small frame. Jack was constantly intrigued by the fact that someone with so much power could seem almost painfully uncomfortable in her station. As if she were the one who didn't belong.

"Hello, my queen"

"It's very nice to see you this morning, Jack," the queen replied.

She then looked at the tall, slim figure standing near a desk on the opposite side of the room.

"Please excuse us, Father. We can finish going over those requests this afternoon," she said.

The dowager king bowed his head out of respect for his daughter before submitting to her request.

"Good day, King Silas," Jack said.

King Silas did not respond or acknowledge Jack as he walked past him to the door. The treatment was nothing new, but it still stung.

Jack fell silent not knowing what to say next. He was the one who was summoned after all.

"My father is old-fashioned. I apologize for his behavior."

"There is no need for an apology, my queen."

Queen Rayvn opened her mouth as if to argue her point but closed it again and looked down at her still fidgeting hands.

"I asked you to come here because I need your help."

"Of course, my queen. Anything you request is law."

The queen visibly flinched at this.

"I apologize, Queen Rayvn. I did not mean to—"

"Please," she replied, looking at his face. "There is no need for you to apologize, Jack. As I said, I need your help with something. I need you to retrieve a wayward. She lives a few miles south of Austin. Her name is Autumn West, and she must be safely and quietly delivered to me."

The queen took a breath and turned away to gaze out of the window. The sun shone in creating an auburn halo around her coils of dark hair. Funny how Jack had never noticed this before. He had always assumed the queen was named for her dark black hair but in reality, her hair was a deep dark red.

"May I ask my queen what is this wayward's crime?"

Hopefully, she wasn't being violent with her domestic partner. If she was an abuser, Jack would have to send Sage to deal with the situation. He could never do what he had to Clay to a female. Maybe she had simply stolen something from the magical community. The property could be returned with an apology after a severe talking to.

"She has committed no crimes against the bakazi. She needs to be made aware of her heritage before her transition."

The queen stuck a hand into a pocket on her dress and pulled out a piece of paper.

"I was visited by the elder, Vervina, about two weeks ago. She had a vision of this young wayward," the queen said, revealing a printed black-and-white photo of a young woman. She was kneeling next to a small boy with a toy truck in her hand. A firetruck. The boy was beaming as he admired what was obviously a new toy.

Though only her profile was visible, Jack could see she was beaming right back at the little boy. For a moment, Jack felt his heart fall out of rhythm. Probably from the display of caring. Jack had seen far too little of that caring in his own life.

"Forgive me, Queen Rayvn," Jack said, "but are you positive that I am the one you wish to send? I don't know a lot about the little ones."

"Little ones?"

"Yes," said Jack. "If this Autumn has a child perhaps someone else would have an easier time interacting with them. Bonding with the child would be an excellent way to gain the trust of this wayward. May I suggest you send Lucky. He is like an oversized child."

"Oh. No, Jack. You misunderstand. This child does not belong to Autumn. She works at an orphanage called Rainbow House."

"This boy is an orphan?"

"Yes," Queen Rayvn said quietly.

Orphans were a sore subject in the bakazi community. There should always be family to take care of a child.

"We were able to use clues from Vervina's vision to locate the wayward. This photo is from a news article about six months ago at a Holiday toy drive at the orphanage."

Jack eyed the photo again, and once more, his heart skipped a beat.

"May I ask, my queen, what vision of this wayward did Vervina see?"

"I can only tell you that she is important for the future of our race."

Chapter Two

Like most afternoons, Autumn said goodbye to her kids with secret handshakes or hugs before heading to log out of her computer, grab her things, and go home. On Fridays, she made sure to fill the purple plastic candy bowl on her desk. She left her door open over the weekend and the kids knew they were allowed one piece of candy per day. She should probably stick to that rule, too.

Autumn popped a kiwi-flavored Hi-Chew into her mouth and headed out into the warm evening air. Other parts of the country were still cool in the spring but in central Texas, the weather was a bit warmer. That was fine with Autumn. She loved this time of year. It felt like the world was waking up from a long hibernation.

When she was little, she planted a vegetable garden with her mom every year. They would plant cucumbers, greens, bell peppers, and tomatoes. Autumn couldn't wait to see the first sign of life poking its green head out of the soil. She also couldn't wait for her mom's famous fried green tomato BLT. It tasted good enough to be famous, anyway. These memories never failed to make her smile. They also reminded her of how much she missed her mom. Something as stupid as a road rage accident had changed her life.

After the accident, Autumn did as she was taught. She hid and waited for her mother at the edge of the forest near where the car had gone into the water. While she waited, she said the prayer her mom taught her.

"Reveal me to the one which protects. Help me in my time of need," she whispered the prayer over and over again until her eyes burned with exhaustion.

The next morning, a stranger found her. He introduced himself as Reece and said she was on his land. The man took her to a hospital to be checked out and then disappeared. That was where a male nurse and a gray-haired social worker told her that her mother was dead and that they would find her a nice family to stay with. Eleven-year-old Autumn ran away from two foster homes before ending up at Wings of Hope Home for Orphaned Youth. Orphanages as a whole don't sound like fun places to be but for Autumn, this was her safe place. Her English teacher, Ms. Brown, and her art instructor, Mr. Keene, made the old gray building feel like a home. It was her village for a time and Autumn wanted to pay it forward to kids like her. Rainbow House allowed her to do that by teaching art.

CHAPTER TWO

As usual Autumn had to park across the street about half a block away from Rainbow House in front of The Church of Fellowship and Mercy or CFM for short. There were always people coming and going from the building. The church was very involved with the community, including Rainbow House. She first met Reverend Adams at the Holiday fundraiser for Rainbow House. He insisted she use the brightly lit church parking lot for safety.

Autumn's phone dinged, pulling her out of her thoughts. Reaching into the side pocket of her purse, Autumn snagged the phone.

It was a text from Kamara.

Out of make-up wipes. Can you stop on the way home?

A hand grabbed Autumn suddenly as she attempted to step off the curb to cross the street.

She tried to pull away but stopped as a truck sped past without ever tapping the brake. Autumn got a quick glimpse of long blond hair as the driver rushed by.

"Watch where you're going," said the deep voice of a stranger.

"Oh my god," Autumn said over the sound of her own heart pounding.

"That crazy asshole in the truck came out of nowhere. He didn't even tap the brake. He's gonna kill someone if he doesn't slow down." Autumn closed her eyes and took a calming breath. "Thank you for stopping me when you did. You saved my life."

The stranger stayed silent. His gaze was fixed on his hand wrapped around Autumn's arm. He seemed to be lost in thought.

"Um hey. Are you okay, sir?" Autumn asked. "I think it's safe to let go now. I promise I will look both ways this time," she said with a smile.

"Yes," he said, finally letting go. "You seem to be out of danger for now. And please call me Jack."

Autumn looked at her hero's face for the first time and almost drowned in his eyes. They were dark blue with a splash of aqua surrounding the pupil. Such a beautiful and interesting trait. Like living art.

"Jack," she said, still unblinking.

She tried to pull her eye away but between those stormy blue eyes, that five o'clock shadow, and that full bottom lip...Wow. He was something else. The stuff fantasies were made of.

"I- um I- my name is Autumn," she stammered.

When had she developed a stutter? And when had her body started buzzing like a downed power line?

Autumn looked down to break the eye contact. She should not be objectifying this man. The good ones were always taken anyway but damn a girl could dream.

"Thank you, Jack. I have been really accident-prone lately and if you hadn't grabbed me when you did, I would be a pancake right now."

"Accident-prone?"

"Yeah, it's like I touched a bad luck charm or something."

"What type of bad luck?" Jack asked with genuine intrigue.

"Well other than nearly becoming a skid mark right now, I almost got crushed by falling books at the library, hit my head in my front yard, and blew two tires in the past three weeks."

"Hmmm. That is strange."

"Yeah. Like a curse, right? Hopefully, you've just helped turn my luck around. Anyway, I better get going. Thank you again, Jack."

"Of course. Be safe," Jack responded.

Of course, Jack thought. Of course, she was Autumn. He was still picking his tongue up off the sidewalk. This wayward knocked him on his ass and he could not stop staring at hers as she crossed the street.

He decided to start his search for Autumn at the orphanage, hoping he would catch her there. He spotted the female walking down the sidewalk in his direction. In the late afternoon light, he could see the feminine sway of her hips. They moved like waves in the ocean. He was almost hypnotized by it. The closer she came the more entranced he became. When he heard the truck engine revving a tingle started at the back of his neck. He saw the woman's intended path and knew what would happen without intervention. Jack had to increase his speed to get to her before she stepped off the sidewalk to cross the street.

He made it just in time to grab her but when he touched her arm, he felt *it*. The tingle spread through his body like a shock wave. That wave was followed by a healthy dose of lust and something else. The burning in his chest was back but he didn't want to hurt Autumn. His inner demon wanted to possess her. He had nearly thrown her over his shoulder and flew them both to his cabin. He would have to ignore his lust if he was to complete this mission. And he would complete the mission for his queen, but he might need help to get it done. Jack pulled out his cell, dialed the number, and waited as it rang.

"What's wrong?" said the concerned voice on the other end of the line.

"I need your help," Jack replied.

"Meet me at Base in ten minutes."

"I'm already there."

After the drive home, Autumn couldn't wait to shower, slip into her PJs, and get some rest. All the way home she couldn't stop thinking about Jack. Those eyes would probably follow her to bed.

CHAPTER TWO

When she walked through the front door, she could hear the bass notes of "Body" by Megan Thee Stallion coming from the bathroom. Kam was pregaming for the club tonight.

"Make-up wipes," Autumn groaned.

With all the excitement she'd forgotten to stop at the store. Her friend was a social butterfly in every way. Social because she made friends easily and the butterfly part explained itself as Kamara gave her best diva walk into the living room.

"What do you think?" Kamara asked. "Is it too naked or just naked enough?"

Her wavy purple hair was slicked into a high pony and matched her electric lavender heels. When a girl had features like Kamara Shaw she did not hide behind hair. Not to mention the 'thick thighs save lives' she was serving in her well-fitted black and white floral romper. Kamara was beautiful.

Autumn never felt beautiful in all of her twenty-five years. Cute, sure. She was no ugly duckling, but she wouldn't call herself beautiful. Her dark brown eyes were a little big for her face, but her lashes were nice and thick. As much as Autumn loved the curls she inherited from her mom, they were the true definition of unruly. Her dark coils would never slick down. Instead, Autumn's hair was a thick cluster of tight curls that did whatever they wanted most of the time. And if anyone dared try to tame her locs with a slicked-back style there would be hell to pay in the form of frizz.

"You look great. I'm so sorry, Kam, but I forgot to stop for make-up wipes," Autumn said, heading toward her bedroom.

"No big deal. We can stop on the way. Do you need help finding something to wear?"

"No," Autumn replied with a sigh. "I'm sorry. I just don't feel like going out tonight."

"No ma'am. You said you would come out with me. No take-backs. You need a night out. Come on girl. First round of shots is on me," Kamara said the last part in a sing-song voice.

"Maybe next weekend," Autumn replied.

"Didn't you tell me that last weekend? And the one before? Come dance with me," Kam said, winding her hips to the beat of what was now "Have Mercy" by Chloe.

"Come on, Autumn. It will be so much fun. Besides, you are too young and too gorgeous to be in the house every weekend."

"I'm really tired, Kam. Raincheck, okay?"

"Fine but next weekend you are coming out with me. No excuses. I'm putting you on notice, Autumn West. And I will be especially hurt if you say no." Kamara made sure to stick out her bottom lip and flash puppy eyes in Autumn's direction.

Autumn took a deep breath and exhaled knowing she had no other choice. "Alright. You win. I could use a little fun after today. Just not tonight. Next weekend I'm down."

"Wait. What happened today? Was your boss mad that you were late? I told you he's not gonna fire you. I think he has a little crush on you."

"No, Kam, it's not that. I... I almost got run over by a truck in front of Rainbow House today."

"What? Oh my god, Autumn. Are you alright? Are you hurt? Why didn't you say something?"

"I'm fine. This guy came out of nowhere and pulled me back onto the sidewalk just in time. I guess my luck is changing."

"Yeah. Thank goodness," Kamara said as she walked over to Autumn and pulled her in for a hug.

"I just need to rest, you know. Prepare for the adrenaline crash."

"Of course. I'll turn the music off so you can rest," Kamara said, stepping out of the embrace.

"Let me go change and start some tea," Kamara said.

"No tea. I'm fine. And no burning sage, either. Go have fun."

"It's yarrow, not sage, and I am not going to leave you alone."

"Kamara, I want you to go have fun. I'll be asleep in half an hour anyway. No need for you to stay and babysit."

But Kam already had her box of tea and herbs in her hand.

"No ma'am. You can have your alone time, but I'll be in my room if you need some company. No matter how late it is, okay?"

"Okay, Mom," Autumn responded mockingly.

Chapter Three

Jack arrived at Base to find Carver busy in the kitchen making dinner. Every member of the household liked to eat. A lot. They all took turns with the cooking, but Carver was a culinary genius. No one was better with a blade in the kitchen or a fight.

Jack walked over to the large black quartz island and took a seat on one of the five bar stools.

"Smells good," Jack said.

"Thanks," Carver replied, looking up from his perfectly chopped potatoes and carrots long enough to grab the olive oil and give the veggies a healthy drizzle.

"Look, I'm sorry I've been in a shitty mood."

"You wanna hug it out or tell me what you need my help with?"

Jack chose the latter, of course.

"It's about the private meeting I had with Queen Rayvn yesterday. She gave me a mission."

"A solo mission?" Carver asked, absently arranging the veggies on a shallow pan.

"She never specified I had to complete the mission alone and there is no way I can now."

"Why? What's the mission?" Carver asked, finally placing the vegetables in the oven.

Instead of answering the question, Jack stood and headed toward the large stainless steel refrigerator.

"Do you want a beer?" Jack asked, opening the metallic door to retrieve two bottles. Without waiting for a reply, he handed one to Carver.

Carver accepted the beverage but did not open it. Instead, he sat his bottle on the black counter and looked at Jack expectantly.

Jack uncapped his bottle before raising it to his lips. The beer was refreshing but probably not strong enough for this conversation.

"She wants me to retrieve a wayward for her. A female named Autumn West. According to the queen, she's important to the future of our race. The queen wants the female brought here and protected for the time being."

"That sounds easy enough for one man. This should be like a grocery pickup for you. We investigate waywards all the time. Why do you need my help?"

"I can't do it alone. Not this time."

"Should we call in Lucky or Sage?"

"No."

No way would he let Lucky get close to Autumn. Lucky was always reliable in a fight, but he had a thing for petite brunettes. One time Jack walked in on Lucky with a pretty brunette stretched across his bed. Her hands were tied to the headboard and some kind of metal bar was attached to her ankles to keep her legs spread wide. Lucky was kneeling on the bed near her head with his junk in her face and she did not seem to mind.

"You and I can handle this without involving anyone else, but she won't be safe with me alone," Jack said, before draining the rest of the bottle.

"I found her today outside of her job. She was not paying attention to where she was walking and nearly got hit by a truck. I'm not so sure it was an accident. I grabbed her just in time but when I touched her—"

"What happened?"

"When I touched her, I felt... I'm pretty sure I felt the pull," Jack said.

"The pull?"

"The mating pull, Carver."

"Jack that's... We can't. Are you sure it wasn't just lust? But even if it's lust—" Carver shook his head. "This is not some human barfly or club girl. She's a wayward and she is important to our queen!"

CHAPTER THREE

"I know. Shit! I know. It should be impossible, but I also know what I felt. My body felt like it was being electrocuted when I touched her. The only way to stop it is to get inside her and I know I can't do that, but my damn zakari is strong wants her, too. She has no idea who or what she is and when she finds out, she is not going to look at me with anything other than fear and disgust. Just like the rest of them."

"They do not all hate us," Carver said, finally uncapping his bottle of beer. "But if you give in to whatever this is they might. One of us mating with one of them is forbidden, Jack, and letting your zakari half have her could kill the girl. It's dangerous. If your emotions are out of control and your dark half wants her it may not wait for her to agree. You shouldn't be alone with her."

"I won't give in. I don't know why I feel this, and it doesn't matter anyway. All that matters is completing the mission. I can track her down, but I need you to retrieve her."

"Okay. I will help you, but if the wayward is in danger, it might be smart to have someone watch my back. You can cover me from afar. Once I make contact, you fly out of there. I'll get her to the queen."

Jack knew he shouldn't see Autumn again. He might be able to fight his bakazi side, but the other half of him was a lot more aggressive. Still, Carver made a good point and Jack agreed because there was no other choice. The queen's request was law.

The elder, Vervina, walked into her home office. She never spent much time in this room only using the small writing desk to pay bills. There was a gorgeous carved mahogany bookcase along the back wall. It was filled with many types of books. Most were over a century old.

She walked toward the bookcase and grabbed the one she needed. It was a dark green leather-bound copy of Grimm's Fairy Tales. On the cover was an illustration of a living forest. Trees with scary faces beckoned the unaware to their fate within. It did not hold the collection of blood-curdling fables that one would assume. This page held knowledge that could change one's destiny. Instead of *once upon a time,* this printed work began with an incantation.

Power of the shadows come forth.
Find this vessel worthy
and grant your power within.

The first time Vervina read those words aloud a bright green light grew up from the floor and snaked its way around her body. It seemed to be examining her for the worthiness she proclaimed. Once the light coiled itself from her ankles to her neck, it started to tighten its hold. The embrace grew so tight it robbed Vervina of oxygen. The room grew dim and just as she drew what was sure to be her last breath, the green light slid down her body, back into the floor and disappeared. She was gasping for life and breath when she heard a voice calling her name. She looked toward the open doorway, but no one stood there. Again, she heard her name. The voice seemed to be coming from all around her, but she could not find the source. The dark green cover made a loud thump as it banged against the desk. The pages began to ruffle and again she heard the sound of her name. It came from the book. The incantation had worked, and the book was offering her all the power written on its magical pages.

If there had been another way, she would have pursued it. Unfortunately, time was running out and she was desperate to find Autumn West and protect the future of the bakazi.

The wayward girl's fate was yet to be determined but she wouldn't live in the dark for much longer. Waywards were named because they chose to depart from the ways of their kind. Walking away from the foal. The reason for walking away was not important. Some were second or even third-generation wayward by now who knew nothing of the bakazi but were called wayward just the same. In the case of this particular wayward, she was ignorant of her heritage because of something else. Autumn was magically spelled and hidden away from the bakazi as a child, but the magic was running out and the time was coming for her return.

Vervina closed the book and returned it to the shelf, having memorized the spell she needed. The gold words on the green spine ensured no one would know she possessed the Opus of Ash. Legend said the Opus of Ash was produced by a powerful family of witches, the Masinas, hundreds of years ago. During the siege to rescue kidnapped bakazi females, the Opus was used to lock the portal to Madalie, trapping most of the zakari in the alternate realm. Before the Masina witches sealed the realm, zakari could come and go as they pleased. Now most were stuck there but there were whisperings that some zakari found a way to sneak through.

Magic always had a back door.

The book was lost or stolen not long after it was used for that infamous spell. It had gone through several channels before falling into Vervina's possession. In the wrong hands, the book could cause all types of destruction. The Opus of Ash was said to interact with the magic of whoever possessed it. Light magic became an unstoppable force for good but dark magic became nearly apocalyptic. But accidents could happen with any magic, which is why she was hesitant to use the Opus.

Vervina was careful about the spell she chose this time. She sought only a way to communicate without being detected by others. No one could know about the conversations. If the wayward was found by those who were currently seeking her it could be disastrous.

She left her office and went upstairs. The spell called for submersion. Because whatever magic surrounded Autumn

CHAPTER THREE

was weakening, Vervina came closer to her target than she expected the last time she tried a submersion spell. The spell inserted her into one of Autumn West's dreams. Vervina was so close. The girl was reaching out for her in the river when something ended the dream. Vervina assumed it was the last remnant of a protection spell. She only had to wait a little longer, before it completely wore off and she would be able to lead Autumn to her destiny, fulfilling her own in the process.

She ran the water and added the necessary herbs. She shed her clothes and exhaled as she entered the bath. The warm water on her skin encouraged her to continue. Once she was submerged up to her neck, Vervina closed her eyes again and slid completely underwater. Vervina was a seeker, not a siliana. Telepathy was not her natural gift, but the spell would grant her access to that power. She needed to be calm to communicate telepathically. All magic was tied to emotion. She tried her best to clear her mind.

Your Highness. Vervina reached out with the help of the spell. *The girl has been found. Autumn West is alive and well for now. However, I believe the spell I used to make contact with her is causing some adverse effects. Probably because she has not transitioned yet. Her powers are growing, but her ignorance is dangerous.*

Vervina waited in the cooling water for a reply.

Bring her to me. whispered a disembodied voice.

As you wish, Your Highness. Vervina replied.

Chapter Four

After a long week of bad luck, it was finally Friday again. Not only had Autumn managed to set off the smoke detector at home, but she also caused the same thing at work. That's the last time she'd let one of her students, talk her into making s'mores, no matter how puppy dog-like his eyes got. Of course, the fire at home happened while trying to make coffee so maybe she should just stay out of the kitchen for a while. Or maybe she needed a vacation. Lately, she couldn't focus on simple tasks without getting distracted or making a mess. These crazy dreams were happening more and now she was hearing voices. If she didn't manage to relax soon, she would need to call a therapist. Hopefully going out tonight with Kamara would help her unwind.

Get dressed up, have some drinks, and dance away the worries.
Autumn wiggled and moved her feet to the beat in her head.
"Oww!"

CHAPTER FOUR

CRASH!

A drawing one of the kids gave her would need a new frame now. While she limped over to grab her trash can her boss poked his head into her office.

"Autumn? You alright?"

"Yeah, Allen. Just practicing for tonight."

Allen's brows furrowed in confusion.

"I'm going out with a friend to do some dancing. Guess I'm out of practice." Autumn laughed.

"You sure you're alright?"

"Yeah, I'm good. Probably a little bruised but I'm good," Autumn said, rubbing her thigh.

Allen lowered his brows in suspicion for a moment before continuing the conversation.

"I was on my way over to give you this," Allen said, holding up a colorful plastic bag.

"Hi-Chew?"

"For your desk. I know how the children like them. It's great the way you connect with them."

"Thank you, Allen. I'll add these to my bowl before I leave today. Actually, is it okay if I head out thirty minutes early today?"

"Can't wait to put on those dancing shoes, huh?" Allen asked, giving a quick spin.

My dancing shoes are probably covered in dust.

"I'm sure you can shake it off."

"What?" *Had he just answered her...thoughts?*

"The dust. Shake that dust off your dancing shoes and you're fine to leave early today. See ya Monday."

"Oh yeah. Thanks, Allen."

Autumn had no idea how she got home. She didn't remember any stoplights or turns. Her mind was busy trying to explain how her boss heard her thoughts. That wasn't possible. It had to be a coincidence. Right? *Either that or I'm a mutant who can project thoughts.* She laughed out loud at the thought while stepping out of her car.

Autumn entered her house and was greeted by the sounds of Rihanna telling her to "Work, work work, work, work, work." That's exactly what she planned to do tonight. No more thoughts of supernatural craziness.

It had been about six months since Autumn put on a pair of heels. At Rainbow House, cute shoes were a quick way to twist an ankle while playing tag. She preferred a comfy pair of sneakers for day-to-day. There was definitely dust on her club clothes, but it would be fun to go out dancing with her bestie.

When Autumn got to her bedroom, Kamara was already pulling options out of her closet. Kam couldn't wait to turn her into a black Barbie doll. Autumn negotiated an oversized rock band t-shirt dress, which Kamara insisted be paired with thigh-high boots. It was never too hot to wear boots in Texas and the three-inch heels were surprisingly comfortable. To finish the look, Autumn pulled her hair back in a low loose pony to show off the ripped design at the shoulder and the boot accentuated the rips at the thigh. Comfy and cool. She liked the look. It was no surprise that a few tendrils escaped before she finished securing the style.

Kamara chose a pair of black shorts with a black lace corset covered by a black jacket. Her purple hair was down in its natural, soft, curly state tonight. Gorgeous as usual.

"You look great, Autumn."

Autumn dropped her hand from the gold ring on the silver chain around her neck.

"Maybe you should tuck your necklace in tonight. You know you can't trust fools in these streets."

Autumn grabbed the familiar piece of jewelry and stuffed it into her neckline.

"Alright. Let's go."

About an hour later, Autumn and Kamara walked into Club Lavender.

Purple lights swirled around the first floor. Bodies swayed to the heavy bass of the music. Austin was known for its trendy nightlife spots, but Lavender was outside the city limits. It was hard to believe such a popular club was on a two-lane road in the backwoods. The DJ was on a platform to the left that looked large enough for a live band. To the right, a long-padded bench lined the wall with a small table and chair placed every three feet or so for additional seating. Behind the bench was the stairway to the second floor.

"I know where I'm headed first," Autumn said, nodding toward the bar.

"Shots! Shots! Shots! Good idea," Kamara agreed as they started to weave their way through the sea of people on the dance floor.

Two vodka shots later Autumn felt a tingle down her back as if someone caressed her. She turned around looking for the asshole who tried to cop a feel, but no one was there. Still, she *had* felt something.

"Autumn?" Kam called over the music. "You okay?"

"Yeah," Autumn said, touching the spot where the gold ring on the silver chain was hidden. "I just... It's nothing. It's just been a while since I've been out."

"Oh, well let's go shake the rust off." Kam grabbed Autumn's hand and headed back to the dance floor.

Three bass throbbing, waist-winding, hip-shaking songs later, Autumn still could not shake the tingle down her back.

"I need to get some water," Autumn said into Kamara's ear so she could be heard over the music.

"I'll come with."

"No. You keep doing your thing. I'm a big girl. Besides, the cutie in the hat is checking you out," Autumn said, pointing to the tall cutie in a San Antonio Spurs cap.

"Have fun."

CHAPTER FOUR

Autumn just needed a moment to shake off the weird feeling. Plus, the dance floor was packed, and she wanted to get some air. She had no idea where she was going, she just had to get away from the crowd. As if on auto-pilot, she walked toward the seating area. She continued past the padded bench to the staircase, feeling pulled to the club's second-floor bar. The loft-style second floor provided a bird's eye view of the dance floor below. She could see Kamara slow grinding on the Spurs hat cutie and it looked like she already caught the attention of another man who was tall, dark, and hot as hell. His dark, curly hair was pulled back from his face, and he seemed to only have eyes for Kam. *Lucky Kam.*

The tingle in her spine was spreading down her legs and she was starting to feel a bit lightheaded. Autumn stepped back away from the rail and turned to head for a seat at the bar. Instead of a clear path, Autumn hit a brick wall and stumbled backward against the railing. Her boot heel rolled, and she braced for a humiliating fall, but the crash never came. In a blink, she was pulled forward and pressed against the brick wall again. This time she felt a hand against her spine and the tingle spread to the rest of her body.

Autumn craned her neck up to look at the person she ran into. She was used to guys being taller than her five-foot-five frame, but he had to be over six feet. Six-two if she had to guess.

His dark blond wavy hair fell in front of his eyes like a curtain. But beyond that wavy veil were the most seductive and unique pair of blue eyes staring down at her. They seemed to be lit from within.

"Jack?" It was strange seeing him again. And again, she was in need of assistance. "I need to sit down," she said, palming her forehead to try and stop the room from spinning.

The hand on Autumn's spine pressed her even more firmly against him before sweeping her up into the cradle of his muscular arms.

"What are you doing?" Autumn squeaked.

"Taking you someplace to sit down. You seem a little shaken."

"I'm fine."

Jack took his time striding through the club, looking for a spot away from the crowd.

The tingles were now centered on a very specific, very warm, spot on Autumn's body. This man had once again flipped a switch with his touch. *Damn, he's fine*, Autumn thought. Maybe she would get lucky... uh *be* lucky, too.

Too quickly, Jack found a bench against the wall and sat her down gently.

"I don't know if you remember but we met the other day. You saved me from being roadkill."

"Of course," he responded, pushing his hair away from his face to reveal his shaved sides. "Autumn, right? Are you hurt?"

"No. Just a little dizzy."

"Can I get you something to drink?"

"I'm just drinking water," Autumn said.

CHAPTER FOUR

"Alright," Jack said with a small smile. "I'll get you a bottle of water."

"Sure, I would like that."

Autumn couldn't look away from that smile. She wanted to bite his juicy bottom lip. How was she so attracted to this man? It had been over a year since her last boyfriend, and she was not looking. Men were not high on her list of priorities, and none had ever made her feel like this. She wanted to dry hump the man right here on their little bench. What the hell was wrong with her?

Jack returned after a few minutes with two bottles of water and a straw. *How thoughtful of him to ask for a straw*, she thought. Jack had been nothing but a gentleman to her. He would not be okay with her straddling his thighs until she... *no. No ma'am.* Where was this coming from? He is a human being, not a battery-powered joystick.

"Thank you," Autumn said as he handed her a bottle along with the straw. She grabbed the straw between her lips and took a long drink, trying to cool her body.

"So do you live around here?" Autumn asked lamely.

"No. I'm here on business."

"Oh, cool. What kind of work do you do?"

Autumn noticed Jack's gaze on her mouth and immediately licked her lips.

"Security," Jack answered, his voice deepening.

"Like a bodyguard?"

That would explain the hot body.

So hot.

"Something like that."

"Do you like what you do?" Autumn asked, trying to ignore her body's response to this beautiful man. She used her straw to take another sip of cold water.

Jack's blue eyes met her brown ones. The corner of his mouth turned up in a smirk.

"It is all I'm good at. I have never really thought about whether I like what I do. I simply do as I'm expected."

Autumn thought there was a hint of sadness in his answer.

"I'm sorry. It's not any of my business. I don't get out much to talk to people my age. I work with kids, so I sometimes forget what filters are."

"No problem. I'm glad I ran into you again," Jack replied, his voice low and smooth.

Autumn bit her lip, trying to control her urges. She didn't want to let lust for this man override her good sense, no matter how tempting he was. But as Jack leaned closer to her, she couldn't help but be drawn in.

"Can I be honest with you, Autumn?" Jack said, his lips dangerously close to hers.

Autumn nodded, unable to speak.

"I don't want to talk right now but your mouth fascinates me."

Jack slowly leaned in and pressed his lips to Autumn's. Her body sparked as if it were on fire. Her core was throbbing to the beat of her heart. She could feel herself getting wet just from a kiss. As the kiss deepened, Autumn's mouth opened in a silent invitation for Jack to explore, and he did. He darted his tongue in and out, stroking her own. His warm wetness teased and then flicked over her lips and along her jaw.

Soft and sweet.

Autumn wasn't sure if those were Jack's thoughts or her own.

"Oh my god!" Autumn gasped, her hips bucking as she felt Jack's mouth move to her neck.

"Jack."

"Mmmm, I bet you taste good," Jack murmured against her skin.

"Oh god. We have to pause this," Autumn breathed.

Jack nibbled at her neck before pulling back to look at Autumn's eyes.

Autumn swiped a few tendrils and tried to breathe normally.

"Fuck," Jack groaned.

"Don't," Autumn insisted. "I liked it. I like you, Jack. I'm just... Maybe we should get to know each other a bit better first."

Jack moved around on the bench next to her, making no secret of adjusting himself.

"I would like to get to know more about you, Autumn. It's just hard— uh difficult to think right now," Jack said. "So. Kids huh?"

"Kids?" Autumn asked, still struggling to clear the lust and think straight.

"You said you work with them."

"Yes. Yeah. Art. I teach art. I love what I do. Kids need grown-ups who will listen and look out for them. I know what it's like to not have that. It's important."

"Yes. I know how important it is for a kid to have someone look out for them, so they have fun just being a kid. Do you have fun with your kids?"

"Oh yeah." Autumn laughed. "Those little people are crazy. We have a lot of fun. Speaking of fun, I need to head back to my friend, Kamara," Autumn said gesturing toward the dance floor below.

"The young lady with the purple hair?" Jack asked. "I saw you dancing with her before, and it looks like she is talking with a friend of mine now. I will walk you down. Maybe we can all go somewhere to eat and talk some more."

"Okay."

Jack had every intention of staying away from Autumn, but she found him on the second floor of the club. She headed straight for his location, as if she felt the pull, too. She was attracted to him. He could smell her arousal. It attacked his senses and overwhelmed him. When she wrapped those heart-shaped lips around her straw, he could only imagine one thing. It was too much for him to resist in the moment. He wanted Autumn West and a part of him would do anything to have her. To be with her. To possess her. Mating with any of the bakazi was not allowed but mating with a wayward was a huge no-no. Especially this one. She was ignorant of her heritage. It would not be fair to her. Not to mention she was important to Queen Rayvn. Still, why would she have come to the second-floor bar when there was a fully stocked bar on the first floor? Would the universe be cruel enough to make his mate someone he couldn't have?

Absolutely. Luck had been against him since his conception.

He was only supposed to watch Carver's back tonight. At least that was the plan until he laid eyes on her tonight. Autumn looked even more beautiful than he remembered. Her brown skin glowed in the club's lighting. He had barely been able to take his eyes off her since he spotted her in the crowd. Jack could feel the prickling of the pull along his skin, so he escaped to the top floor. Carver was supposed to make his move. Ask Autumn to dance and get her to talk to him. Instead, she had headed in Jack's direction and Carver was in what looked to be an intense conversation with Autumn's friend. Shit. She looked pissed.

The purple-haired young woman was headed for the front door by the time Autumn and Jack made it to the dance floor.

"Where is she going?" said Autumn. "I'm so sorry Jack. I gotta go."

And just like that, he was watching her walk away again.

Chapter Five

It was a good thing Autumn sobered enough to drive because Kam was in no shape to get behind the wheel.

"Who was that?" Autumn asked, breaking the long silence.

Kamara shook her head and continued to stare at the road ahead. She had not said a word since leaving Club Lavender. Silence after a fight was out of character for Kam. She was never the silent type. She always shared her emotions. The good, the bad and the angry. Why was she so shook by Jack's friend?

"Did he say something disgusting and weird?"

"No," came Kamara's flat reply. It was the first word she had said in nearly half an hour. *Progress.*

"Did he touch you or something? Gurl, did he grab you? 'Cause we can turn around right now and go back to kick his ass!" Autumn continued speculating and getting herself worked up in the process.

"Nobody puts their nasty, dirty, disgusting hands all over my best friend without permission. I will punch him in the throat, and you can kick him in the balls. If Jack tries to stop us, he can get kicked in the balls, too."

The part about kicking Carver in the balls got a little smile from Kamara, which was good enough for Autumn. Not that she wouldn't follow through on her threats but her first priority was to make her friend feel better.

"Come on, Kam. Tell me what happened."

Kamara took a deep breath and glanced over at Autumn before looking back at the road again.

"We dated," Kamara finally said. "I felt— I thought I felt something for that asshole. He made it clear that I was not what he wanted. I was probably just some exotic fantasy to check off a fucking list. Literally. He ghosted me after we had sex for the first time. Well, lesson learned. I'm sorry I ruined your night out, Autumn."

"What?" That was not what Autumn expected at all. Kamara had never mentioned any of this.

"First of all, you did not ruin my night. Second, when did you date him? I thought you hadn't been in a serious relationship in... ever."

"I haven't been and that six-foot piece of shit is the reason why. I know you know me as the good time girl but the reason I haven't been in a serious relationship in a while is Carver."

"We met at a café on fifth," Kamara said. "I was sitting alone having tea and the best strawberry brownie in the state of

Texas. It was so good I had to close my eyes and enjoy it. When I opened my eyes, he was staring at me from his own table. I smiled and he smiled back. Then he walked over and asked if he could join me. Normally I would have declined but something about his eyes and that smile just pulled me in. We talked for a long time. He told me he likes to cook. Savory not sweet. Anyway, we hit it off and he asked to take me out on a real date. Then one date led to five dates and five dates led to sex."

"Okay," Autumn managed while trying to process this new information.

"It was incredible. That man treated me like a queen. A filthy, nasty, dirty queen," Kamara said with a giggle.

"Kamara!"

"Well, he did. Multiple times but that morning he was gone. The no-good bastard. I thought... well it doesn't matter what I thought obviously because he didn't feel the same."

Kamara had never said anything about having romantic feelings for anyone. For all her talk of hot guys and clubbing she never brought anyone home with her. Autumn had never seen Kam with anyone who wasn't a friend or coworker.

"The offer still stands," Autumn said.

"What?"

"The offer still stands. We can turn around right now and go whoop his ass. How dare he treat you like some brown-skinned curiosity? You don't even have to get out of the car. I will kick him in the balls for you. You can be the lookout and the getaway driver."

"Gurl," Kam replied between laughs. "Who would bail us out of jail if we both get locked up? Besides if I drive all the way back to Club Lavender, I am getting a couple of licks in. Not licks like *licks* but you know punches."

"Yeah, nasty I know what you meant. And I know something else, too. Bastards of a feather flock together. Jack is probably just like Carver. Trying to live out some kind of urban fantasy. He will never get a whiff of this good-good."

Both girls erupted in laughter.

"What the fuck was that, Carver?"

"Kamara," Carver responded quietly.

"I know her name. She's Autumn's friend but who is she to you? More specifically, why does she hate you?"

"I spent some time with her a few summers ago. We... dated."

"Okay. What did you do? Why did she break up with you?"

"She didn't break up with me."

"Carver, after that shit show at Lavender I am not in the mood for any more bullshit."

He let Carver take the lead and they had not only walked away without Autumn, but they had managed to piss off her friend. Carver never behaved like this in the field. There had to be an explanation. There better be one hell of a good explanation.

"The queen commanded that Autumn be found and safely delivered to her and you may have blown that mission over a woman. Tell me what is going on between you two. Why have you never said anything about her if she meant anything to you?"

"I had to walk away from her. You should learn from my example," Carver answered with a pained expression on his face.

"Why?" asked Jack.

"She's bakazi. Kamara is a wayward just like Autumn."

"What?" Jack ground out through clenched teeth.

"I had no choice but to break up with her before the feelings got stronger. Our bastard fathers really screwed our lives. All because their own females were cursed with infertility."

"Are you sure she is bakazi? Did she admit this to you?"

"No, she didn't admit it to me because she doesn't know what she is. She healed me. While we were—"

"What?"

"It was after a sparring match with you. You landed one of your monster kicks to my back. You know that was a lucky kick, right?"

"Sure, it was, Carver. Continue."

"I was distracted because I had a date with Kamara. Anyway, I hadn't completely healed when I met up with her that afternoon. Let's just say she was as excited to see me as I was to see her."

"You fucked her."

"Watch your damn mouth, Jack." Carver was in Jack's face with his knife clenched at his side in less than a second. Carver always carried a blade and no one in the squad was more deadly with an edge weapon.

Jack slowly raised his hands in the universal sign for surrender and looked Carver in the eyes. He had never seen his friend this aggressive. If he tried to match Carver's mood nothing good would happen. Besides if Carver felt for Kamara like Jack felt for Autumn, he could understand the guy's anger.

"I am sorry, brother. I meant no disrespect. I am only concerned," Jack said. "I need to understand your feelings for Autumn's friend."

An eerily calm look crossed Carver's normally bright green eyes.

Carver took a step back and put away his weapon but maintained eye contact with Jack.

"Just drop it," Carver said before walking away.

Chapter Six

Rayvn stared at the white letters against the night-mode black background on her e-reader. Reading was her nightly getaway. All day she answered emails from bakazi in need. Those who lived on the land came and went with questions for their queen. They asked for things as simple as a blessing for their union to more complicated things like whether it would be safe to visit certain regions. The bakazi who lived on the forty-plus acre tract of land came over from the continent with the royal family. It was like their own little village.

She was glad to help her people, but she enjoyed this time to unwind. For a few hours in the dark when the big house was quiet, she could relax and lose herself in a fictional world. Unlike her own story, this fictional one was guaranteed to have a *happily ever after* with a little spice along the way.

"That's my good girl," he whispered, pushing into her from behind.

Rayvn was suddenly too warm for the layers of bedding she usually enjoyed. "That's probably enough for tonight," she said to her empty room.

Her room was filled with beautiful furniture, but no love or joy lay within its walls. When she was alone in the dark it felt more like a cage. Yes, there were more important things than love but recently her loneliness was causing restless nights and dangerous thoughts.

Rayvn walked over to the handmade dresser beside the door. It was her favorite piece of furniture in the mansion. It had belonged to her mother and made Rayvn feel like she was still watching over things. The insides of the drawers still smelled like her mother's perfume. She sometimes spoke out loud in front of the dresser as if she were having a conversation with her mom. Traditionally the ascending queen would take the master bedroom along with whatever furnishing she wanted to keep. Rayvn decided to keep her old bedroom. There was comfort in the familiarity. Her father made the dresser a gift to Rayvn to celebrate her coronation.

Rayvn ran her hand across the top of the dresser. The wood felt smooth and cool to the touch. "I wish you were here. I have so many things I wish I could talk to you about. Am I doing the right thing with Autumn West? I cannot talk to Dad about this, you know how old-fashioned he is when it comes to our traditions," Rayvn sighed.

The next breath she took was filled with the scent of vanilla smoke.

CHAPTER SIX

"Hello, Pretty Wings," said a voice in the dark.

Rayvn gasped at the unexpected greeting. That voice always caused the need to squeeze her thighs together.

"You can't be here," Rayvn said breathlessly.

"I'm here for you," came his dark reply.

"What does that mean?"

"What would you like it to mean, love?"

Rayvn stayed silent, refusing to play his stupid guessing games. How dare he show up here after all this time? Where was he when she needed him? When she desperately needed the cover of his arms?

"Your safety has recently come into question, Pretty Wings."

Years ago, she had begged the universe for this man's protection. Well, he was not exactly a man, but the fact remained that she needed him, and he abandoned her. She had been so stupid to trust him.

"I have around-the-clock guards. When could I possibly be in danger? This is more of your bullshit. I asked you once to take me away and keep me safe and you refused. Now all of a sudden you want to be a white knight. I don't believe that, Mikael."

Finally, he moved out of the shadows and Rayvn's heartbeat accelerated. Familiar almond-shaped eyes glowed in the dim light. Most of the time his eyes were like brown cracked glass. Veins of black pigment snaked their way outward from his pupils giving the shattered effect that had intrigued Rayvn from the beginning. Right now, those amber eyes glowed. He was having trouble keeping his emotions in check.

"I never claimed to be a white knight. I prefer to be your avenging demon." He grinned, showing off his sharp K9s to punctuate his statement with the swagger that only Mikael could manage.

Rayvn was reminded of the sweet sting of those fangs against her breasts. Every dark trait Mikael possessed attracted her to him. The white zakari marking on the side of his face and neck nearly glowed in contrast to his dark skin. Her fingers twitched with the need to trace each swirling line, from his neck up to his smooth head and then back down to his broad shoulders and chest. Rayvn squeezed her eyes shut before speaking again.

"Your vengeance is several years late," said Rayvn.

"I came for you, remember? Fourteen years ago, I offered my vengeance against the ones who hurt you. I wanted to drown them in their own blood, but you told me to leave, so I did." Mikael swiped his hand over his bald head in frustration.

"I could feel your fear. I thought it was directed at me but now I know what you were afraid of, Pretty Wings. I know the secret you kept. I should have stayed." he said shaking his head.

"I did not come to you now to make excuses for my inaction. Just know that if I could have taken away the pain with my own life I would have."

Rayvn knew he was telling the truth. If she had been honest with him ten years ago, she wouldn't have had to be alone.

"You can't be here, Mikael. You have to leave before someone finds you in my bedroom. I can hear my father in the hall now. If he comes to check on me and finds you here—"

"I know what Silas is capable of, and you know what I am capable of. That's why I came to you. I wanted to talk to you first, so you understand what has to happen and why I have to be the one to make it happen."

"What are you talking about? Just tell me why you're here."

"I'm here for your father's life, Rayvn. He has been in contact with some of my peers."

"Your peers? You mean zakari?"

"He's been shopping for an enforcer. An assassin, Rayvn."

"My father wouldn't know how to make contact with demons of any kind, and he doesn't have any enemies to assassinate anyway. Even if he did, why wouldn't he use the kin squad to get rid of them?"

"The kin squad might take exception to killing his intended target and enforcers are ruthless. An enforcer won't question a kill order as long as they are compensated. You know that as well as I do. As for knowing how to make contact, your father has lots of connections as the former king of the bakazi. Many of your people have more loyalty to him than to you, my love. Any of them would jump at the opportunity to prove their loyalty to him, no matter what it meant."

Rayvn felt her stupid heart skip another beat from him saying the word love. Her brain knew he didn't mean it. Mikael lusted after her and was extremely possessive of her, but that didn't mean love. Zakari *couldn't* love. Her father made sure she knew that. She needed to get her own heart under control.

"My father is the most traditional person I know. He knows the laws better than anyone. He would never do what you are accusing him of."

"Silas is a smart man. He wants her dead and he wants it done right."

"Her? Who are you accusing my father of trying to have killed, Mikael?"

"The future of the bakazi race. Autumn West."

The name dropped like a boulder and so did Rayvn's heart.

"I will not let that happen. Silas will die by my hand and no other."

"No. How would he find her? I have a guard looking for her right now with orders to bring Autumn safely to me."

"I don't think it would be wise to bring her here. If you get in the middle of this, you could be hurt. Leave her to me. I can protect her until Silas is taken care of."

"No, Mikael. Haven't you done enough to fuck up my life? Now you want to kill my father, too! Just go. Forget your crazy conspiracy theory. Autumn West will be protected."

Mikael stepped closer to Rayvn. His hand reached toward her face until a long finger tilted her chin up so he could look into her eyes. She didn't shy away from him. His vanilla smoke scent wrapped around her like a cozy blanket. She closed her eyes and savored the aroma in spite of herself.

"Do you trust this guard who's looking for her?"

"Yes, of course."

Mikael closed the inches between them and kissed her lips. His mouth brushed hers so lightly she wasn't completely sure he touched her at all. Then the tip of his tongue poked out to caress her lips before he sealed their mouths together. His lips were warm and demanding. He deepened the kiss and she opened for him. After all this time she still responded to him in a flash. She craved this warmth. If she was honest, she craved *him*. She wanted more. Mikael's hands encircled her waist to pull her body closer. The feel of his hard body reminded her of how well they fit together. His big hands slid down her hips and around to caress her ass.

Rayvn whimpered under his touch. Her control was slipping. In a few minutes, she would be bent over the closest flat surface with her legs spread for him.

Too quickly, Mikael pulled away from her.

"Order your guard to keep Autumn hidden until this is over. He can watch over her until I'm able to finish this. When Silas is dead, I will reclaim what belongs to me."

Mikael took one step back before disappearing in a black mist and Rayvn knew she was the thing he meant to reclaim.

Chapter Seven

Jack's long blond braid slapped against his back with every quick stride. The wind brushed against his shaved sides as the scenery moved by. His chest moved up and down at a steady pace despite the high-intensity workout.

After the shit show at Club Lavender, Jack had no idea how to get the mission back on track. Things were going great until Carver screwed the pooch. Even if he recognized Kamara, why did he have to approach her? Did he really think that she would forgive him after what he did? Did he think she would want him once she knew the truth of what he was?

Now another three days had gone by, and Jack was in a worse position than where he started. He had to regain Autumn's trust. He had been so close.

Autumn returned his kisses at Club Lavender, but she would never accept him once she knew the truth. She *could* never accept him. She was bakazi and he was not. At least not to those who made the laws. Besides, how could he get Autumn West to trust him when he didn't trust himself? He needed to clear his head and come up with a new plan. That's how his run had begun. He ran across the acreage that housed their little bakazi village so to speak. While the mansion was front and center it was flanked by several smaller houses. Bakazi families were welcomed to live on the land in peace if they wanted. It was a custom passed down from their ancestors. The bonus here was that this particular parcel of land sat on a vein of blue stone known as llanite. The blue stone was better than a security fence and didn't take away from the view of unspoiled nature.

Jack pulled up as a ball rolled into his path and a little bakazi girl came running after it.

"Watch out kid!" Jack yelled, only succeeding in making the little one freeze in place. Unable to completely stop his momentum, Jack skidded into the kid. Dust rose all around them, stinging his eyes as the little girl fell to the ground with a thump.

"Shit— er shoot, kid. Are you all right?"

He extended his hand to help the kid stand up and quickly pulled it back. Maybe she shouldn't stand. She could have a spinal injury. She'd fallen kind of hard. She should stay still and wait for him to find a tari.

The little girl sat up, swatting at the dust on her blue and yellow striped shirt.

"You should not move, girl. Your back could be broken."

The little girl's eyes widened before her tiny face scrunched up and a sob escaped her mouth.

Jack had no clue how to stop this or what set her off. Maybe it was the pain of a broken bone or maybe it was simply being in his presence. What would his Autumn do? No, not *his* Autumn. Just Autumn. How would Autumn West calm one of the little ones she worked with? He needed to channel her abilities to put kids at ease. She said she had fun with kids.

Jack held his hands out, palms facing the girl, and took several steps backward. He knelt on the ground and tried to speak to her again.

"Sweetheart? Can you tell me your name? My name is Jack. Like a Jackfruit or a Jackfish."

The girl sniffled.

"Have you seen a Jackfish before? They swim really fast."

Jack put his palms together and made a side-to-side zigzag motion while he sucked in his mouth and cheeks like a fish.

"Jackfish," she said with a smile, mimicking his hand motions.

He kept up the funny face until the girl laughed.

"My name is Sky, like... " the girl pointed a tiny finger upward. "I'm seven years old." She smiled.

"It's nice to meet you, Sky. I apologize for running into you, but next time you need to look both ways before crossing the path. Are you sure you're alright?"

Sky nodded and stood to her feet.

"Yes. I'm fine. Are you okay?"

Jack's brow rose and he was speechless for a moment. This tiny bakazi girl was concerned for him. A six-foot-three half-demon.

"Sky. Come back into the yard, baby. Leave the nice man alone."

A young woman with short dark hair waved the child in her direction.

"He's a fish, Momma."

The young woman eyed him warily.

"Go on, listen to your momma," Jack said, handing the red ball to Sky.

"See you later, Jackfish."

Jack got back to the barn-dominium after dark. He ran until his legs were sore and he lost track of time but now he had a plan. He decided to go to Autumn. He would meet her outside Rainbow House and apologize for his stupid friend. Then he would invite her to have a drink. He would ask her to tell him more about the kids she worked with. Talking about them seemed to make her happy and Jack would enjoy hearing the stories. Once she was comfortable, he could feel what her response to being magical might be. Not every wayward took the news well. It was better to test the waters, so to speak. If she was open to the idea that the supernatural might be real, then he could tell her the truth. If not, he would need a new plan.

Jack grabbed a protein bar and water bottle out of the pantry on the way to his room. He started the shower and ate his makeshift dinner waiting for the water to come to temperature. When steam started to billow out of the doorway to his private bathroom, he stripped down and stepped into the shower. Exhaustion from the long run was starting to set in, pushing Jack to make quick work of lathering and scrubbing his big body. The water massaged his scalp and shoulders while he untied the long braided mohawk. After the shampoo and conditioner routine he stopped the water and dried off. Pulling on a pair of sweatpants, Jack headed for his bed.

The next thing he saw was Sky in her blue and yellow striped shirt standing out in the darkness. She was playing with her red ball. Why was she outside in the dark alone? When her eyes locked on Jack, she smiled and raised her hand in greeting. Jack waved back and Sky continued kicking the ball down the path toward him. When the thing rolled into his foot, he bent to pick it up and return it to his little friend but when he raised his head it was to a horrifying sight.

A tall figure in dark sweats and a hoodie grabbed the little girl. Sky's feet kicked as she was suspended off the ground by the stranger. Jack dropped the ball and ran toward the girl. Her captor made no attempt to escape.

"Put the girl down!" Jack demanded.

The captor spoke the same words at the same time but kept his head down. The hood and moonlight threw shadows over his face making him an even more ominous sight.

"Let her go!" Jack and the captor said in stereo.

A dark chuckle rumbled from the hooded figure and Sky began to disintegrate and blow away like ashes in the night.

"No!"

Jack rushed the man knocking him to the ground, but the chuckle only grew louder. He pounded into the stranger with both fists. The man did nothing to defend himself and continued to laugh. Then the man brought his hand up to remove his hood between blows and Jack froze in place.

"This is you, Jackfish," he said mockingly.

"I am you. You are me," the thing said, pointing a finger from itself to Jack.

"We are we," it laughed.

Its face was identical to the one Jack saw in the mirror every day and the words were terrifying.

"You think she wants to be your friend? You think she's not terrified of you? They will never accept you. You will never be one of them. Just give up and give in to me. Pure instinct."

Jack jumped to his feet and moved cautiously away from the thing. Now a few steps away, he watched the personification of his demon side. The thing's eyes glowed, illuminating its face in blue light. It had his straight brows, his jawline, his lips but was it really him?

Before Jack could respond, a strong wind blew out of the trees. It was the kind of thing you felt during hurricane season as a precursor to the big storm. Lights like fireflies started to twinkle in trees and he took a step toward the glittering forest.

He turned his head back to his evil twin in time to see him fade away into nothing. He didn't mist out like a zakari or fly out like a bakazi. He disappeared like a fading memory. Solid, then transparent, then gone. Before Jack could process it all he heard a voice come from beyond the trees.

"Hello?"

It sounded like a female and the voice was familiar. The wind continued to blow against him but pulled him in at once. Without another thought, Jack walked into the forest. Everything about the scenario was calling to him.

"Hello?" the sweet voice said again.

Whatever lay on the other side of the trees was put there for him. It was where he was supposed to be. Not on this dark dirt path battling with himself. He belonged inside that twinkling forest.

Chapter Eight

Three days after the run-in at Club Lavender, Autumn couldn't stop thinking about Jack. She tried staying busy. She pulled every weed she could find in the flower bed. That made her think of rolling in the grass with Jack. She asked Kamara to show her how to make macaroons. She pictured Jack sucking cookie batter off her fingers. Today she tried exercising after work, but in the middle of doing mountain climbers, she managed to conjure an image of a sweaty, shirtless Jack hitting a punching bag. That hallucination led to the cold shower she was just leaving. Autumn tied her hair up like a pineapple on top of her head and slipped into her favorite PJs. No one was going to tell her that twenty-five was too old for the Power Puff Girls. Those cutie pies kicked ass. The light tank top that showcased the flying trio was thin and cool which was a necessity in the Texas heat.

Autumn adjusted the red ruffled shorts that complimented Blossom's red bow as she climbed into bed. They were a little junior but sometimes a girl just wanted to feel girly. Jack called forward all the girly energy in her body, but she had to forget about him. Girl bros before man hoes. Kamara was her best friend, so it didn't matter that Jack gave her butterflies with the sound of his voice. It didn't matter that he made her heart race with a simple smile. So what that his eyes made her panties melt. Who cared that his lips looked soft and kissable? They *were* soft and kissable. She would never kiss those soft full lips again, and Autumn told herself it was fine as she closed her eyes and rubbed her thighs together until she fell asleep.

When Autumn opened her eyes she stared at the stars in the night sky. Beautiful. The stars seemed to be brighter and the sky darker. She sat up and rubbed her face. A warm breeze ruffled her curly hair. When had her bed been moved outside?

"Hello?"

She was dreaming and she was rarely alone in these things.

"Is anyone here?"

Autumn's full-sized bed was in a forest of cypress and oak trees under the stars. No doubt this was the same forest she dreamed of over recent weeks. This was, however, the first time she found herself in her bed in the forest. It was also the first time she noticed fireflies among the trees. Rustling beyond the trees caught Autumn's attention. Intrigued but not afraid, Autumn swung both feet over the side of the bed to stand on the ground. She could feel the grass between her toes. How? She should not be able to feel anything in a dream.

"Hey!"

Autumn turned to the sound and squinted at the person emerging from the treeline in front of her.

Long legs encased in low-slung joggers moved swiftly in her direction. He looked ready for bed to her. The closer he came the better the view. A very happy trail of dark hair dusted his lower abs. And oh what wonderful abs they were.

Damn, when I dream up a man, I check all the boxes, she thought.

When he stopped in front of her, Autumn finally could see his face. Blue eyes the color of the sea looked down at her own.

"Jack?"

"Autumn?"

"Wow. I'm having a sex dream about him now?" Autumn mumbled.

"Sex dream?" Jack interjected.

Autumn pursed her lips.

"Chicks before dicks. I promised but he did save my life." She continued thinking out loud. "Who wouldn't want a real life hero? My knight in cotton sweatpants. So what if it's a desperate sex dream."

"Desperate?"

He seemed almost offended. Of course, her dream Jack was the sensitive type, too.

It's just a dream. She should be allowed to break girl code in her dreams. Dreams were supposed to be where you lived out your fantasies and worked out your real-world problems with no consequences.

Without wasting any more time, Autumn reached up to frame his face with her hands. The prickling of his five o'clock shadow sent tingles racing down her arms and caused her nipples to tighten under her tank top.

Jack opened his mouth for a rough inhale and Autumn wasted no time accepting the invitation. She quickly rose to her tip toes and pressed her lips to his. She licked and nibbled at his full bottom lip. Sighing and moaning, she let her pleasure be known.

Then with a deep moan Jack took control of the kiss, pressing his lips roughly to hers with one hand at the base of her skull to accentuate his command. His other hand swept down the side of her breast, skimmed over her waist and came to rest on her round ass, his strong fingers squeezing.

Autumn took this as an invitation to wrap her legs around Jack's strong waist. Her arms were tingling before but now her whole body was buzzing like a hive of honey bees. She couldn't help but shiver even though she wasn't cold. Her body had never felt anything like this.

"Bed," Autumn demanded between warm kisses.

"Oh my fuck," Jack cursed.

After a couple long strides Jack turned and sat on the side of Autumn's bed. Her body was soft and warm wrapped around him.

Jack could feel the wet heat of Autumn's core pressed against his naked waist.

"Stop!" his conscience yelled. But his conscience was a fucking liar. This felt every kind of right. Jack let his finger slide underneath Autumn's red ruffled shorts. The treasure he found there would have brought him to his knees had he still been standing.

"Damn it, you're warm."

Autumn startled. The voice coming from Jack sounded deep and sinister. It should not have enhanced her arousal, but it did.

Jack stood and pulled away just long enough to place Autumn on the bed.

Autumn laid back with her thighs spread begging for his touch. Jack took his time. He started his caress at her feet. He bowed his head to land soft kisses on the inside of both ankles. Slowly his hands moved up Autumn's calves followed by several of those soft kisses. Jack's kisses were so soft that it felt like she was being caressed by butterflies, but his hands were rough. The opposing sensations were driving her crazy. How could she feel so much in a dream? Before she could think about it too much, Jack's lips met her thighs and all she could think about was pleasure.

She arched her back and whimpered as he pumped his finger in and out and in and out. She had never been so hungry for a man's touch. He honestly was a dream lover. And there were no regrets or consequences in a dream.

Autumn started to ride his finger. She was so close to release. So close but Jack's hands were not enough. She could be greedy in her dream, and she wanted more.

"Fuck me, Jack. Fuck me," she whispered.

"Autumn..."

"Fuck me, Jack."

Jack kissed her inner thigh one last time before sliding away from her.

"You do not know what you're asking, little Kipeyo,*" Jack said with a pained look on his face. "If I fuck you now, I will never stop. I'll take every inch of that sweet pussy you're offering and then I'll take things you aren't prepared to give. Things you won't even know I've taken until it's too late. Until we're both damned. You need to wake up."*

"Jack?"

"Wake up, Autumn. Wake up now. Now!"

Autumn closed her eyes long enough to take a deep breath and when she opened them again, she was not in the forest. She was back in her room. The forest and her dream lover may be gone but the effects of the dream remained. Her nipples ached and her ruffled pajama bottoms were soaked.

Autumn reached down to remove her wet shorts and reveal her throbbing sex. She closed her eyes and imagined that her hands were Jack's hands discovering her body. She moved her left hand over her stomach and up to cup her right breast. She imagined Jack's long fingers pinching her already taut nipple and rolling it between his fingers.

CHAPTER EIGHT

"Jack," she whispered.

Meanwhile, her right hand sought the wetness between her legs.

"I wish you could touch me like this."

Two of her fingers swept through the moisture and into her core. Autumn closed her eyes and pictured Jack's face as she started to move her fingers in and out, mimicking the motion from her dream. In her mind, he was still shirtless in those low-riding joggers, and he was breathing heavily. In her mind Jack squeezed his eyes shut as she continued to stroke herself closer and closer to the edge.

"Yes. Fuck me. Yes. Yes. Jack," she moaned softly.

Her mind and body yearned to make him real as she hurried toward her peak. She imagined Jack's tongue swiping a wet trail along his full bottom lip. One big hand swiped his long hair away from his face and held it like a makeshift headband. She wanted to run her hands over those shaved sides and tangle her fingers in the thick hair at his crown.

Jack's other hand was below the elastic band of his jogging pants, and he was no doubt trying to find his own release. When he opened his eyes again, they were glowing, but Autumn was too far into her pleasure to care. Just as her orgasm crashed over her Jack started to growl, and she saw a flash of his white teeth. His sharp... white... fangs? How the hell could she hear him and why the hell did he have fangs?

Vervina wiped the steam from the mirror and stared at her reflection. The fine lines at the corners of her eyes were a reminder that she was starting to age. Her dark brown skin no longer glowed with youth. Bakazi were not immortal. Most lived about three hundred years. Some longer depending on how well one took care of themself. Vervina was over two hundred years old. She never had a husband or children. The bakazi race was her family. They were all her children to love and protect no matter the cost. The right decision was not always the easiest for everyone, but she would always do right by her people.

So, when she was approached with the chance to correct past mistakes that would harm the bakazi she was hesitant. How could any good come from consorting with the enemy? They were selfish types who sought power only to further madness and confusion. But after several meetings, she was convinced.

Vervina dried her body but didn't bother with clothes after her shower. She opened the door that connected the bathroom to her bedroom. The lights were dim, but she could make out his slender form lying on the bed waiting for her. His long violet robes with gold trim were parted to reveal his naked chest.

"Hello, Your Highness," Vervina said.

Silas insisted on formality even in the bedroom.

CHAPTER EIGHT

"Vervina, you look lovely. Come here," Silas said, holding out a hand in invitation.

Vervina complied. Silas had been the king of the bakazi for nearly a century. He loved their people as much as she did. After his beloved Queen Olive passed on three years ago, he deserved to find comfort. It was an honor to share her body with him. Silas was a loyal leader to the bakazi and upheld all the traditions of the past.

She had fallen in love with him while he courted Olive. After being seen in public with Princess Olive, Silas would make his way to Vervina's family home and climb through her bedroom window. She turned down multiple invitations to go out with friends so she could be home for Silas. Her parents assumed she was a shy introverted young lady, and they were right. Only Silas had ever been able to captivate her enough to let him in. He was her destiny. He was always confident and powerful. He would order her to her knees, and she would offer her body and heart to him. She prayed to the universe that he would return her love.

"Sacrifices have to be made," Silas would say.

Olive was to be queen and there would be no better king than Silas, so Vervina put the good of her people before herself. Now her love had returned to her asking for help to deal with a threat to the future of their people. He couldn't return her feeling then but surely now he could.

"Kneel, Vervina. Hands and knees."

Her body shivered at the sound of his command as she slid gracefully into position. She had practiced the pose many times to please King Silas.

"Yes, Your Highness."

She knew he would love her this time. She'd done everything he asked, up until now. All these years of faithful service to her people would be very attractive to Silas. He had to see more than the physical. He would hear her out and she would finally get her happily ever after.

"I love—"

"Do not speak, doll. I have a better use for your open mouth."

Vervina followed his orders. She knew he valued more than just her body. Silas always considered her opinions. There would be time to discuss their plans for the wayward later.

Chapter Nine

Autumn had been distracted all week. She couldn't get that dream out of her head. She thought about talking to Kamara about it more than once this week but changed her mind after doing some research. Her search results said that what she was experiencing was lucid dreams. In a lucid dream, a person could feel and see things almost like in real life. Half the population has experienced lucid dreaming at least once but that didn't explain what happened after she woke up. At least she thought she was awake. But if she was awake, how could she possibly have heard Jack? How did she see him so vividly? Why would she picture Jack with fangs? It couldn't be real. She needed to get Jack out of her head. He was driving her nuts.

"Ms. Autumn. We made something for you," said a familiar little voice at the office door.

"You did? Come over here, Millie. Let me see."

The little girl skipped over to Autumn and held out a piece of paper.

"This is you and this is me and Diego," Millie said pointing to the figures on the page.

"Wow! This is great. Did you draw this yourself?"

"No, Ms. Autumn. Diego drew it because he's a really good drawer. He let me color it in though."

"Cause you're so good at coloring."

"Yeah," Millie boasted with a big smile.

"Well, you know I love pictures from my kiddos. Thank you."

"Presents always make me happy," Millie continued, "and I wanted you to be happy instead of sad when you find out that me and Diego are leaving."

"Leaving?"

"We got adopted so we have to leave Rainbow House, Ms. Autumn."

Adoptions were emotional every time. She tried to bond with all the children at Rainbow House, which made them all special to her.

"Oh, Millie. I'm certainly going to miss you both, but this is wonderful news. You and Diego get to have a new home with a Mommy and a Daddy and maybe even a pet."

"Ms. Autumn."

"Yes, Millie?"

"Your eyes are watery."

"Oh," Autumn said, dabbing at her wet eyes. Her chest felt tight. She loved these kids. She didn't plan to ever have children of her own. How could she be a mom? There had been no one to teach her. She had no family. It took a village to raise a child and she would never have that. She always got emotional when the kids left but she never cried in front of them.

"These are happy tears, sweet girl."

Millie gave her a small sympathetic smile.

"Why don't you go play, sweetheart?" Autumn said with what she hoped was a convincing smile. "I'm so happy for you both. I'll find you and Diego before I leave today for some big hugs, okay?"

"Okay," Millie agreed before wrapping her arms around Autumn's waist for a quick squeeze. "See you later."

Autumn was happy for Millie and Diego. They deserved a happily ever after, but it was always hard to say goodbye to her kids.

Autumn reached up to bat away more tears. Her emotions were all over the place lately. As much as she hated to burden Kamara with her problems, she needed her best friend. Maybe it was time to tell her about those crazy dreams.

Autumn picked up the phone and dialed her bestie.

"Hey, Autumn. What's up?"

"I was thinking. Why don't we have a girl's night in tonight? No boys allowed. Except maybe Winston Duke or Ryan Reynolds."

"Those men are fine," Kamara said.

"And safe. Winston and Ryan would never break our hearts or date us to fulfill some kind of stupid fantasy."

"Assholes. Jack and Carver, not Winston and Ryan," Kamara clarified.

"I know. I will stop on the way home for drinks and snacks. You grab the creams, lotions, and potions."

"Potions?" asked Kamara

"Yeah, girl. Depending on how drunk we get I may want to turn Jack and Carver into toads."

They both laughed before saying bye.

After work, Autumn stopped at Cliff's Corner Store to get gas and snacks on her way home. Nothing says *girl fuck that man* like wine, snacks, and a Tyler Perry movie. Then a few hours of yelling, "Kick his ass!" at Winston Duke or Ryan Reynolds might also make them feel pretty good.

"Thank you," Autumn said to the gentleman holding the door for her as he entered the store. The smell of nacho cheese and hot dogs tickled her nose. "Hey Henry," she smiled at the cashier. Henry always worked the night shift. As usual, he had his nose in a biology book. "How's school?" Autumn inquired, heading for the snacks.

"It's challenging. Becoming a vampire is not as easy as Stoker made it seem," Henry replied.

"What?" Autumn asked as the front door chimed and two customers walked in. One headed toward Henry at the checkout counter.

"Becoming a vampire. You know. A phlebotomist," Henry said with a smile before turning away from Autumn to greet his customer.

"Oh. Right," Autumn said as she stopped in front of her guilty pleasure. Hi-Chew was great for everyday chewy goodness but gummy bears were her go-to for a comfort snack. She grabbed the green bag with the trees and six colorful bears on the front.

"Sweet gummy bliss," she whispered to herself and headed for the back corner of the store.

Cliff's kept non-alcoholic beverages in a reach-in cooler along the left and back walls, but in the corner between the rows of reach-ins was Autumn's destination. It was a walk-in cooler where the beer and wine were stored. After the past couple of weeks, she deserved a glass of wine. The front door chimed as Autumn entered the cooler.

"Now what color wine goes with gummy bears?" she asked herself since no one else was around. A pink wine with black and gold lettering on an off-white label grabbed her attention.

"Black Girl Magic Rosé. Yes please."

"Autumn."

Autumn looked around to find the source although she recognized the voice. First Rainbow House, then the club, and now in a gas station's walk-in cooler.

"Jack," she said with a frown and a slightly suspicious gaze. "What are you doing here? I know you don't live around here so..."

"No. I just... I have to talk to you."

"About what?" she snapped.

"Not here. I need you to come with me right now," Jack replied.

"What? Umm no. Why would I do that?"

"Autumn—"

"How's your friend Carver? Kamara told me everything. Are you stalking me so you can do the same thing to me?"

"Stalking? No, I am not stalking you. I just really need you to come with me right now."

"Why?" Autumn inquired as she grabbed the bottle of Rosé.

The cute ones are always crazy, she thought.

"This place is not safe for you," Jack continued.

"Yeah, I'm starting to realize that," Autumn replied, clutching the neck of the bottle like a baseball bat.

"EVERYBODY DOWN!"

Two tall young men were holding very large guns near the front of the store. Both had a long bleach-blond braid and white patches of lost pigment on their grim faces. They didn't need the guns to look scary. Autumn flashed back to the person in the truck who nearly ran over her.

Someone started to scream near the cash register.

"QUIET!" scary guy number one said.

"Oh my god," Autumn whispered.

"We have to go now!" Jack ground out through clenched teeth.

"I know she came in here," said scary guy number two.

Autumn was having trouble comprehending how bad her luck had gotten. *A robbery?*

"Go where? We're trapped in here." Autumn looked toward the frosted glass door. "That is the only way out of this room."

Jack wasted no time.

He grabbed Autumn's hand and pulled her in flat against him.

"That is not the only way. I will keep you safe," he said.

"What about the other people?" Autumn asked.

"Those two are looking for you, Autumn. They won't hurt those people. They can't afford to draw any heat from the police," Jack replied in a hushed monotone.

Jack's big body seemed to surround Autumn in all directions. She could hear his heartbeat. The rhythmic thump was calming in the chaos.

An ice-cold breeze surrounded them. It was as if the air was a living entity.

The thumping in Jack's chest was slowing down. How could he be so calm? They were in the middle of a robbery.

"Take a deep breath," Jack said.

Autumn did as she was told and before she could exhale, they were no longer in the walk-in cooler of Cliff's Corner Market. She was still tucked against Jack's chest. His arms were still wrapped tightly around her but now she was outside.

She could smell the grass. Then Jack opened his arms to let her out of his embrace. He quickly lowered his head toward his shoulder and pinched the bridge of his nose like he felt a migraine coming.

Autumn had to admit she felt a bit strange as well. Her heart and mind were racing. *How the hell did they get outside?* The moon glowed above them. Crickets chirped all around them. They were outside in the woods.

"How?" Autumn said between shallow breaths. "Jack? What was.. how did we... Jack?"

Jack kept his eyes closed tight. The light show behind his lids was not something he wanted to explain right now.

"Jack?" she reached out to touch his face.

Having her so close was calling his demon half to the surface. Her soft curves against his body were the closest thing to heaven he could imagine. He wanted to keep that feeling for himself. He wanted to sink into her warmth until they were one. His body hardened in places he hoped Autumn wouldn't notice and now she was touching his face.

"Am I dreaming?" she asked.

And now he was picturing the dream they shared. *Shit.* The burn in his chest was starting. He had to calm down. Taking several deep breaths, he tried to banish his zakari urges.

When Jack dared to open his eyes Autumn's face was all he could see. Her soft round face made him want to protect her and her heart-shaped lips made him want to kiss her until she was naked and underneath him. Her eyebrows were drawn together. She looked so concerned for him. No one other than his squad had shown concern for him in a very long time. Tingles danced along his jaw and neck where Autumn's hand had come to rest bringing back memories of kissing her. If she kept this up, he would take her here and now.

"Stop touching me," Jack said roughly.

He didn't want to scare her, but he was struggling to fight his other side with her so close. If she kept touching him, they would both be fucked.

"Please," he added.

"Sorry," Autumn said, dropping both hands to her sides. "I was just concerned. What you did...whatever you did just now to get us out of there, did it hurt you?"

"Flying. It's called flying and no that doesn't hurt me," Jack replied as he took two steps back.

"Flying?" asked Autumn.

"Yes. It's like bakazi teleportation."

"Bakazi?"

"Not now. We need to get you to a safe place. Those... people at the corner store were there for you. If they find us, they will kill you. I think they may have tried before. One of them was the guy in the truck the first time we met. I don't know how I didn't see it before. I need you to trust me, Autumn. I'll answer all of your questions, but we need to move."

Chapter Ten

This is not how Jack imagined this night would turn out. He had been replaying the first time he met Autumn on the sidewalk outside Rainbow House. The driver of that truck had bleach-blond hair. Nothing too strange there but the more Jack thought about it the more he questioned whether he had seen the white facial markings that identified saam. Most saam had a pale mask of missing pigment around their eyes. To humans, it looked like a skin condition called vitiligo, but the bakazi knew better. In the human world, it was a beautiful anomaly. In the magical world, the white mask was a warning.

If it was a saam they were not working alone. Saam were simply foot soldiers for someone smarter. They were not known for being critical thinkers. They were bred to be yes men, loyal to the zakari who created them and nothing more. Enforcers were the only exception. They were saam who had no interest in following orders. Some didn't even look like a saam. No white mask across the eyes. As far as Jack knew, enforcers were oddities of nature like black swans or white pandas but not nearly as cute and cuddly. If the driver had been an enforcer, Autumn would be dead. Her ignorance about the magical world made her too easy of a target. As much as he wanted to ease her introduction to the bakazi, he decided to speed things along for safety's sake.

The evening began with Jack waiting for Autumn outside of Rainbow House. He moved up and down the sidewalk for about forty-five minutes and then realized he was not alone. The smell of burned vanilla reached his nose, telling him someone else was watching the orphanage. Watching his wayward. Jack scattered his cells and reformed on the same rooftop as the unfortunate lemming who had been sent to watch Autumn.

Killing the saam helped Jack work off some aggression. He should have thanked the guy before breaking his spine on that trashcan in the alley behind that building but there was not much time for thanks while dropping someone off a roof. Five minutes later Autumn walked out of Rainbow House and started driving while Jack followed unseen in a scatter of cells.

The plan was to go to Autumn tonight and explain everything. Unfortunately, that did not happen. Tonight did however confirm that the saam were after her. And when those two blond turds walked into that corner store, he knew Autumn West was not safe in her world anymore. Somebody wanted her dead or worse and she needed his protection.

He had to explain the truth to her and make her understand that he could keep her safe. At least until he got her to the mansion. Queen Rayvn said Autumn would be important to the future of the bakazi. Confirmation of this threat meant she needed to be under the protection of the entire kin squad. For now, they needed a safe place for the night. Jack was anxious to get Autumn within the safety of the mansion and its blue stone border, but he couldn't risk giving away the queen's location if they were followed.

They walked along an overgrown path into the woods for about half a mile. The path ended at a thick grove of trees. Jack walked over to one of the trees crouched down and placed his hand on the trunk. There was a soft click then a line of trees started to move to the side. A hidden sliding gate was just one of his security features. He had worked hard to hide this place. On the other side of the camouflaged gate stood a one-story cottage. The front porch was raised about three feet off the ground and encompassed the entire front of the building. The arched windows and doorway made the place look like a dollhouse. Scalloped cedar shingles helped camouflage the rooftop just like the front gate.

"Come on," said Jack heading toward the cottage.

Autumn followed his command and walked up the steps behind him.

"You know my roommate is going to be looking for me," she said.

Jack had not thought about that. His only thought in that cooler was to get Autumn to safety. Sure, he could have fought those two but what if she got caught in the crossfire? He would not let any harm come to the woman who chased his nightmares away.

"Your roommate will be taken care of," said Jack.

"Taken care of? What the hell does that mean? If you hurt her—"

"No one is going to hurt anyone. I can have Carver speak to her or you can call her, but you cannot tell her where you are."

"Why not?"

"Do you think Kamara would come for you if she knew there were people after you? That people were trying to hurt you?"

"Yes."

"And if she is the only thing in the way those saam will kill her without a second thought. Is that what you want? You want Kamara to risk her life for you tonight?"

"No," Autumn recoiled.

That seemed to get her full attention. Fear for the safety of others. Good. Whatever it took to keep her safe is what Jack was willing to do.

"Then we do things my way. I can keep you safe and I can keep your friend safe, but you need to listen to me. If Kamara pokes her nose too far into this life she will get hurt. Your choice, Autumn."

Jack put in a code on the keypad next to the entryway and opened the door.

"I'll call her. I don't know what I'm gonna say but she hates Carver, so I will call her."

Jack gave a nod of approval.

"Can *I* at least know where we are? Is this where you live?" Autumn asked, reaching up to hold the gold ring on the silver chain around her neck.

"No," Jack replied without looking back. "I come here to be alone sometimes, but this is a safe house."

"Safe house? As in a hideout? As in witness protection?"

"As in cover for the night," Jack answered.

"I don't understand any of this. Why would anyone want to hurt me? I'm no one important. I teach art at an orphanage. I don't have any money. I have one close friend. I hardly date. This is crazy."

"Inside," Jack said, holding the door open for Autumn to enter first.

Autumn eyed Jack from underneath her lashes.

"Please," he added, motioning Autumn to go ahead of him.

After a few seconds of looking into Jack's eyes, Autumn took a deep breath and walked forward.

"This is it. Everything in my life is about to change, isn't it?" Autumn asked as she crossed the threshold.

Jack did not bother to reply. He knew a rhetorical question when he heard one.

Chapter Eleven

After locking the door behind them, Jack hit the light switch. The cottage was sparsely decorated. A floral couch and matching loveseat formed an L-shape in front of a stone fireplace. It was homey. Under different circumstances, Autumn would have really enjoyed the feel of the cottage.

"You can sit anywhere," Jack said before disappearing down a hallway.

"Can I have some water please?" Autumn asked after a few minutes, breaking the uncomfortable silence.

"Water?" Jack said reemerging.

"Yes please."

Jack walked into the open kitchen area and opened the fridge to retrieve two bottles of cold water. He crossed the short distance to where Autumn stood next to the couch and offered her a frosty plastic bottle.

"Thank you," said Autumn. "I need you to tell me what is going on."

"Alright. I'll explain everything to you. Sit down," Jack said, gesturing toward the couch.

Autumn sat down on the couch and twisted the top of her bottle to open it. She took two sips then looked up at Jack expectantly.

When Jack chose to sit on the loveseat, Autumn was unexplainably disappointed that he hadn't chosen to share the couch with her. None of this made sense, including her feelings.

"We are bakazi."

"Bakazi. You said that before. What does it mean?"

"The bakazi are what you might call fae. I don't like to use that word, but most people are familiar with the Celtic fae folk of Ireland. The bakazi are from Central Africa. We have some of the same abilities."

Autumn's eyebrows popped up.

"Fae?"

"Yes but no."

"From Central Africa?" she asked.

"Yes."

"But you're White."

"There are millions of Africans who look like me, Autumn."

Of course, Autumn knew this. It was a dumb thing to say but she was having trouble processing things. He just called her a faery. This was the real world and magic was not real.

"I know. I just... This is all so crazy. I'm still trying to comprehend how we got out of Cliff's."

"Like I said before, it's called flying," Jack said. "We don't have wings or anything. Mostly we are just people with special gifts."

"If I am like you, what's my special gift?"

"You are not like me," Jack responded more harshly than he intended to. He was something hated, feared, and looked down upon. Autumn, his Autumn was nothing like him. She was warm and beautiful and wanted.

"You are a wayward. Ignorant of your heritage because your parents walked away from the bakazi community. That's why you don't know anything about your heritage. All bakazi can fly and control the four elements: water, fire, earth, and wind. In addition, most have another gift. I think you are a dream walker. After we talked at Club Lavender you came to me in a dream. Do you remember it?"

"Oh my god," Autumn said, hiding her face with both hands.

"It is alright, Autumn. There's no need for you to be embarrassed. Your gift is telepathy and dream walking is a form of telepathy. You can enter a person's mind while they are awake or while they sleep. It is a very powerful gift."

"I tried to have sex with you."

"Yeah," Jack grinned.

"I'm so sorry."

"Why are you sorry? I will never be sorry for that night. Besides, you are new to magic. No one can expect you to know how to control a gift you were not even aware of."

"Gift? Is that what I'm supposed to call this?"

"Bakazi powers are meant to assist nature and our people. It is how we have survived for thousands of years. Yes, these are gifts."

"How can invading someone's private thoughts help them in any way?" Autumn asked.

"There are three types of bakazi. Seekers can see future events. Tari have the power to heal. You are a siliana. Your gift of telepathy means that you have the power to communicate with anyone and anything in nature. It is rare to dream walk, but it has happened with some siliana in the past. I will take you to meet our queen tomorrow. She is the one who requested you be brought here. She says you are important to our people and she must be right if the saam are after you already."

"This is crazy. I'm supposed to believe I'm some magical dream faerie? Even if I do believe you, why did my mother never tell me anything about this? Why would your queen care about me?"

"Siliana bakazi. Not dream faerie. And I don't know why your parents didn't tell you about your heritage. All I know is the queen requested you be brought to her. Her request is law. We do not question it."

"Fine. What type of bakazi are you then?"

"I am something else. Not only bakazi. My powers work differently because of my mixed blood."

Jack held his hand out and curled it into a fist. A fist that started to glow and was becoming engulfed in flames.

"I can manifest the elements, not just control them."

Autumn opened her mouth, but no sound emerged.

Jack unclenched his fist and made a throwing motion toward the stone fireplace. With a woosh, the previously untouched logs started to burn.

"Is that enough proof or should I keep performing ridiculous tricks?"

Autumn's eyes widened.

"How did you... How... how is any of this real?"

"I will explain more but first let me feed you."

"I don't really feel like eating. This night has my stomach in knots."

"You need to eat something, Autumn. I will make chicken and rice for me and rice soup for you to settle your stomach. While we eat, I will tell you about the bakazi."

"Okay."

A faerie? Autumn thought. A fucking faerie? No way. This is real life, not some cartoon. Faeries aren't real. Magic is just for kids. Right? There had to be a rational, non-faerie reason for her dream. The term lucid dream did not explain why she was able to hear and see Jack after waking up that night.

Jack's fork clattered against his plate shaking Autumn out of her thoughts. Too late she realized she had been staring at him.

"Yes," Jack said.

"What?" Autumn managed to tear her gaze away from his mouth to look him in the eyes.

"You were staring at my lips. You either want to kiss me or you're wondering if I really have fangs," Jack replied. "The answer is yes to both."

Autumn sat speechless. Her face felt tight, and she hoped Jack couldn't tell she was blushing. In one night, she had been caught in a robbery, magically teleported, accused of being a faerie, stashed in a safe house with a strange man and now the man had fangs and wanted to kiss her. Autumn shot to her feet so fast that she knocked over her chair. As she started to back away, her foot got caught on the ladder-back dining chair. Instead of dashing the door, Autumn fell to the floor with a squeak twisting her knee in the process.

"Autumn. There is no reason for you to be afraid of me. I would sooner rip my fangs out of my mouth than hurt you with them."

Jack offered his open hand to Autumn to help her off the floor.

She refused, and instead, half crab crawled half scooted her body toward the couch.

"You're a fucking vampire!"

"I'm not anymore a vampire than you are. Vampires need blood to survive. I merely enjoy the taste. It's like French chocolate or an expensive glass of wine. Blood is a delicacy," he continued while watching Autumn pull herself off the floor and onto the couch.

"Am I supposed to just believe you? I barely even know you."

"I did save your life. Twice."

Jack sat on the couch giving Autumn as much space as he could. She was obviously in pain, and he wanted to take that from her if she would let him.

The cabin was stocked with several herbal remedies for pain and injury. He could run her a bath with lavender and rub her injured leg with rosemary and coconut oil. He would bet her legs were soft and warm. He could massage the oil up to her gorgeous thighs then ease them apart and drink from her.

Shit. Rubbing oil on Autumn was not a good idea.

"Maybe this is part of some game you're playing. You think it's fun to play with your food or something. If blood is a delicacy, am I dessert? I bet you can't wait to suck me dry."

Jack's vision went blue, and a low growl started in his chest.

"Mmm. I would love to taste you, but you will not be sucked dry. When I get my mouth on you Autumn you will be soaking wet. Would you like that?"

Autumn's breath hitched. The rise and fall of her chest quickened and she pressed her thighs together.

Jack moved closer, his eyes focused on her like a wolf stalking its prey. Autumn knew it would be smart to escape the predator in front of her. Her brain was telling her feet to move but her feet were not listening. Not only were her feet not listening but the closer Jack moved to her the warmer her entire body felt. All Autumn could do was stare into those hypnotic eyes. His eyes resembled shattered glasses with wisps of black skating threw the mesmerizing blue surface.

"Jack?" Autumn gasped.

This is insane. He has fangs, and glowing eyes and he is growling at me. Why am I not peeing my pants?

Then to her surprise, she growled back.

Jack was on her in the next second.

His lips were soft but demanding on Autumn's mouth. She leaned into his body meeting his urgency with her own.

Jack gripped her thighs and Autumn opened herself to him. He broke their kiss to move his warm mouth and silky tongue down her neck.

Would he bite her? Would she like it?

Autumn felt a tickle in her chest just before producing another growl. *What the hell? Since when was she a growler?*

Jack's head snapped up at the sound and there were those glowing cracked glass eyes again. He peered at her from underneath his thick lashes as if he wasn't sure if she was a challenging predator or delicious prey. He swiped his tongue across his lips and grinned then struck quickly like any smart predator. Before Autumn could react, Jack's hand was around her throat. Not squeezing but forcing her back onto the couch underneath him.

CHAPTER ELEVEN

Jack's fingers tugged at the waistband of Autumn's pants. *Holy shit.* This was hotter than her dream. Her dream that was real because she made it real. Was that happening now? Shit. He was right. She was a fucking faerie and she was doing it again.

Autumn pushed forcefully against Jack's shoulders, twisting and squirming until she fell off the couch and onto the floor.

"Stop," she panted. "Stop." Autumn threw her palms over her face and hoped she could disappear. "I'm sorry. Oh god, I'm so sorry. I didn't mean to..." she said still sprawled on the floor.

"I know. It's okay. I should not have kissed you. I shouldn't even be near you. We need to work on controlling your powers."

When had he hopped over the couch? Jack had been on top of her one minute and now he was nearly in the kitchen. Autumn wasn't sure how he got there but she was glad for the piece of furniture between them. Why couldn't she control her sex drive around this man?

"I was using my powers to control you but I'm not asleep. Am I?"

"We are awake but remember, dream walking is a type of telepathy. You can hear and project thoughts. You planted a suggestion in my mind."

"I am so sorry, Jack. I would never want to force you or anyone else to do something they don't want to do. I don't want this stupid *gift*."

"It's not all on you. I let you into my mind because I wanted to. I wanted what you were offering. I still do but your blood and your body is forbidden to me," Jack responded.

"Why?"

"There are rules among the bakazi. I would never be permitted to touch you in such a way."

"If we are both bakazi why would I be forbidden to touch?"

"You are pure bakazi. I am not. My blood is mixed. Every member of the kin squad is the same. We are spawn."

He said the words with such shame.

"Spawn?"

"Not too long ago, several bakazi females were taken by the zakari. They were made to breed with them to produce a new race. Children like me. When Queen Olive found out where the females were being kept, she sent the royal army to rescue her people. She even contacted a powerful family of witches for help.

"The royal army with all their honor and tradition were like lambs against the zakari. The queen's army was decimated. Some of the bakazi females were able to escape with their young. Others remained trapped and are presumed dead. The witches sealed the Madalie realm but no one knew what to do with the unwanted offspring from their forced unions."

"What happened to them?" Autumn asked.

"Many of the mothers understandably wanted nothing to do with the monsters they were forced to birth. There are stories that some of the females took their young and left the community because they knew the young would never be accepted by the bakazi or safe from the zakari. The handful of soldiers who made it out alive delivered any unclaimed young to Queen Olive. She decided to take us in."

"She adopted you all?"

"No. We were raised to be warriors. The royal army had lost most of its fighters. The monarchy was left gravely unprotected. The bakazi people would never have accepted us as one of them, but the queen could not bear to kill us. Instead, rules were put in place. It is forbidden for any of the spawn to lay with a bakazi. I can never take a wife or father a child for fear of passing on zakari genes. We named ourselves the kin squad because we are the only family that we will ever be part of. You are safe with me, *Kipeyo*."

"You called me that before. What does it mean?"

"It means butterfly. Beautiful to look at but best left untouched."

Chapter Twelve

Standing under the warm spray of the shower, Autumn's head was spinning. Jack told her about the bakazi. She saw the magic for herself, and still couldn't believe it. Had both her parents been bakazi or was she half human? That could explain why her father was not around. Maybe he was living his best fae life while her human mother struggled to feed them both. But why hadn't her mother ever said anything? Surely, she knew these powers would manifest at some point. Unless her dad never mentioned his magical genes.

The cloud of steam in the tiny bathroom shook Autumn out of her thoughts.

She turned the water off and pushed the glass door to the side to step out of the tub/shower combo.

Jack had given her a t-shirt and shorts to sleep in. They obviously belonged to him. The shirt fell just above her knee and even with the drawstring fully engaged the shorts kept sliding down. The wood floor was cold against her bare feet as she hurried across the hall to Jack's guest room. Autumn closed the door and slipped out of the oversized shorts. She pulled back the fluffy comforter and shoved her feet under the covers. She settled her head on the pillow and closed her eyes.

Rain fell on Autumn's face as she lay on the soft grass. It felt good, like a cool spray from the sprinklers on a warm day. Frogs croaked what had to be a happy song. Autumn opened her eyes to enjoy the sound for a minute before sitting up. Another vivid dream. Hopefully a pleasant one.

The purple flowers surrounding her in the field moved and swayed under the weather. As with most dreams one minute you're doing one thing and the next you're driving a car.

She cruised along the familiar route listening to early 2000s pop music. The trees swayed and moved as she passed them by. The interior of the car looked familiar, but it wasn't her blue Honda hatchback. This was her mom's 1998 Honda Passport and she was driving toward her childhood home.

Just as she realized where she was headed, a large animal darted out into the roadway.

"Shit!"

She jerked the steering wheel to the right to try and avoid the fury roadblock and the world turned upside down. The crunch of metal and glass mixed with her own scream was the last thing she heard before everything went black.

A loud knock intruded on the darkness. The banging got louder, and Autumn tried to open her eyes. She fought against the darkness, not sure if she was awake or asleep.

"Ma'am?"

KNOCK! KNOCK!

"Ma'am?"

KNOCK! KNOCK!

"You alright?"

"Is she okay?" said a second voice.

Wake up, Autumn thought.

"I think she's unconscious."

"Is she hurt?"

Wake up.

"Ma'am."

Wake up.

Autumn's eyes flew open wide. She was still dreaming. The car was right side up and she was sitting in the driver's seat.

"Ma'am, are you alright?"

"I'm okay," Autumn responded but as she looked in the direction of the voice a tall thin figure stood unmoving outside her car door. The figure was covered in a long, hooded robe which left no clue to their identity.

"Who are you?" Autumn said as she exited the car.

The figure turned at an inhuman speed and grabbed Autumn by the throat.

"Abomination!" yelled a distorted voice and that was when Autumn noticed the knife in his hand.

"No. Stop!" she screamed, striking out at him. Suddenly this dream felt too real, and Autumn was in a fight for her life. She screamed, kicked and punched her attacker.

But something had an invisible hold on both her wrists. An unseen force pinned her arms to the car door behind her and there was no way to escape.

Wake up!

"Noooo! Get off me!"

"Autumn. Listen damn it. You have to wake up. Open your eyes."

On command, Autumn's eyes flew open wide. Jack's worried face floated above hers. His hands held her wrists beside her head against the mattress.

"Jack," she cried. Her voice sounded like a prayer to her ears.

"Yes. I'm here. Are you okay?" Jack replied slowly releasing his grip. "I heard you screaming. When I got through the door, I realized you were fighting a nightmare."

Jack released Autumn's wrists and sat back on the bed, giving her room to breathe, but Autumn didn't want space. She threw her arms around Jack's neck as tears of relief ran down her cheeks. She had not known him very long but she knew he was a safe place. She knew she was safe in his arms.

"I was so scared," she whispered nuzzling between his neck and shoulders. The closer she got to him the closer she wanted to be. He smelled like he had just taken a shower but there was something else underneath. His scent drew her in until she found herself nuzzling his neck.

A prickling feeling started just below her knees, and she realized that somehow, she had managed to scissor Jack's torso with her bare legs. She nuzzled closer.

The tingle, the same one she'd felt in the club, worked its way up Autumn's thighs as she started to press her body against Jack's naked side.

"If you are alright, I will go back to my room." Jack said, easing Autumn's head off his shoulder.

"Don't go." Autumn said nuzzling her body closer to his.

"You aren't wearing panties."

"They were dirty."

"Autumn."

"You smell good. Why do I get like this with you? I've never been this brazen with any other man."

"Do not mention other men to me right now. It makes me want to mark you as mine."

"How would you mark me?" Even as she asked, she knew the answer wouldn't matter. A primal part of her wanted to be marked by Jack and she wanted to mark him in return. She wanted his hands on her. She wanted his mouth on her. It was all she could do to not rub herself against his body and purr.

"Show me," Autumn said.

In the span of a second Jack reacted. Thrusting his tongue into her mouth and pinning her to the mattress with his powerful upper body. She was surrounded by him. She couldn't draw a breath without inhaling him. Autumn arched her body trying to get closer.

CHAPTER TWELVE

When Jack broke the kiss to look at Autumn's face, his blue eyes resembled cracked glass and they glowed down at her. The look on his face could not be described as anything but hungry. His other side was close to escape, and she wanted to break his control. Autumn raised her face close to Jack's and she took his full bottom lip between her teeth. When she started to suck a moan escaped from Jack's throat before breaking the connection.

"Shirt off," he demanded, rising to his feet.

Autumn scrambled to her knees and obliged.

Jack's pants disappeared faster than she could register. Everything about him was oversized. His biceps twitched. His wide smooth chest pumped up and down to the rhythm of his rapid breaths. Autumn's gaze wandered lower, searching for that happiest of trails that she liked so much but it was hidden behind the most perfect penis she had ever seen. Not that she had seen a lot of them. But of the three she had seen in person, this one got first place. She couldn't take her eyes off it as she started to crawl to the edge of the bed. Autumn's steady hand reached out to catch a bead of moisture that clung to the swollen head. She brought the treasure to her mouth and moaned at the first taste of him.

"You're so damn beautiful," Jack said. "I feel whole when you touch me like that. Do you want me, Autumn?"

"Yes," she sighed.

"I won't hurt you, but I want you to scream for me. Let me know if it's too much."

He flipped Autumn onto her back with her head at the edge of the bed.

"I want you, Jack. Whatever that means."

"Open."

Autumn knew this would be rough, but she wanted it. She wanted him just this way. She opened her mouth, Jack guided himself inside and she clamped her lips around him. As his hips moved slowly back and forth, he reached for Autumn's soft breasts. The feel of his rough palms and the sensation of him moving in her throat was more than enough to set her off. Her body bowed up off the mattress and she moaned around Jack's cock, but he was not done. Jack placed his palm on her throat and squeezed her jaw, silently demanding more pressure around his shaft. Autumn accepted the challenge. Jack fed himself into her until she could hardly breathe. He pinched one of her nipples and fireworks exploded behind her eyes. The world went white as she found her release. She gasped for breath as Jack left her mouth and walked to the side of the bed. The mattress dipped under his weight.

"Get that ass in the air. Has anyone ever had this ass, Autumn?"

"No. Nobody," she answered moving into position.

Jack moaned and rubbed her ass before nipping at one of her cheeks.

She was more than ready to have him inside her any way he wanted. But instead of that swollen head, she felt a slick tongue between her legs.

CHAPTER TWELVE

Jack was on his back with his head between her thighs, making a meal out of her. He feasted on her body. Autumn started to wiggle against his mouth. She cried out. Greedy and overstimulated at once. A vibrating sensation forced a yelp from her mouth. Jack was humming into her body. No, not humming. Purring. Growling.

Jack hooked his arms around her naked thighs making it impossible to move no matter how sensitive she became. Daring anyone to take away his new favorite treat.

"Please," Autumn begged, unable to form more words than that as the impending climax caused her brain to glitch.

"Jack!" she screamed as another orgasm crashed over her.

He moaned and drank down her pleasure but did not stop.

"Oh god, Jack!" she panted using her few seconds of clarity. "Inside."

Jack continued to lick and kiss. Then she felt a light scrape against her lower lips.

"Fuck!" Autumn shouted over Jack's low growl.

He let go only long enough to move his mouth over to kiss her upper thigh. The growl grew louder as Jack punctured her thigh with his fangs and started to drink from her. His tongue lapped up any drop that dared try to get away.

The sharp sting and the firm wet suction drove Autumn screaming over the edge once more.

"Jack," came a hoarse whisper.

Please, I need you inside me, Autumn spoke into Jack's mind.

The suction stopped. Jack changed his grip on her thighs and jerked her body down his own until they were perfectly aligned.

Autumn took Jack in her hand and guided him inside her. With the multiple orgasms paving the way, she had no trouble accommodating his impressive size.

Autumn sighed as Jack's hips started to move like tides on the beach. His rhythm was slow and almost hypnotic at first. She closed her eyes to enjoy the ride. Jack's hands found her hips and used them to steer her toward what would certainly be another orgasm.

Autumn knew that even on top she was not in control. Her arousal climbed even higher at the thought. She wanted to be at his mercy.

Jack hammered harder and faster into her core and Autumn met his motion with her own.

"Cum for me again," Jack commanded.

Autumn's body reacted immediately as if it belonged to him. Her eyes popped open as the orgasm took over every muscle in her body. Head thrown back, fingers clenched, and spine bowed, Autumn called Jack's name over and over as she tumbled over the edge. Jack buried himself deep and stayed unmoving while her core clenched around him. Once the rippling subsided Jack began a slow retreat. He pulled back until only the thick head remained inside her then rocketed himself deep.

"Are you protected?" Jack groaned.

CHAPTER TWELVE

"What?"

"I'm going to cum inside you. Tell me you are protected."

Autumn clenched around his shaft. She had never done that before, but she wanted it now. She wanted this experience with Jack.

"I'm on birth control."

"Good," he said pushing into her faster this time while Autumn continued to milk his cock with every stroke.

"Do you want me to cum, *Kipeyo?*

"Yes."

"Ladies first," he said sliding deep inside her once more.

Autumn gasped as her body reacted to his command. Her orgasm triggered Jack's explosion. His warm essence filled Autumn and she wanted to stay with him like this for hours.

Autumn collapsed onto Jack's chest without bothering to separate. They both worked to control their rapid breathing. Her eyelids suddenly had weights attached to them. Maybe Jack would hold her all night and keep the bad dreams away.

"Stay," Autumn whispered as she drifted off to sleep.

"I belong to you," Jack responded.

Chapter Thirteen

When Autumn woke the next morning, she heard voices coming from the living room. Voices plural. Should she stay hidden in the bedroom listening to the conversation or make her presence known?

Autumn decided listening for a few minutes would be the best decision.

"I trust you, Jack," said a female voice.

An annoying feeling close to jealousy caused Autumn's chest to tighten. Why would she be jealous? Jack was not hers. He made it very clear that he would never be hers, not even in her stupid telepathic dreams. That wouldn't change just because they slept together.

"I belong to you" was the last thing he said to her before they both fell asleep. But what did that mean? Maybe it was like *I aim to please.* No need to read too much into it. It was simply a nice response to someone asking to cuddle.

"Thank you," Jack replied, "but are you sure I am the best person for this job? I called Carver earlier this morning. He's going to bring enough food for the next two days. Perhaps he should stay and look after Autumn."

"Jack there is no one else I would choose to watch over Autumn. You're well-trained, compassionate, and disciplined. Besides, your cottage is well hidden in these woods. This will be a good place for her to learn."

"May I ask, Your Highness, is everything okay? You came here with no guard, and you don't seem like yourself."

"I don't always take a guard on my morning runs. You know that. Don't worry about me. I have the others to keep me safe. You keep Autumn safe while she explores her powers. I will return for her soon."

"Yes, my queen."

Queen? She was the one who had Autumn brought here. She needed to meet this woman. She needed to ask questions.

Autumn rushed out of the bedroom and down the hall wearing Jack's t-shirt.

When she turned the corner into the small living room she froze.

The woman speaking to Jack was absolutely beautiful. Her height was similar to Autumn's five-foot five-inch frame. Her dark green jogging set showed off her slim build. Her dark red hair was in two braids that draped over her shoulders to rest on her chest. The woman swiped at a piece of curly hair that had escaped its binding. On her hand was a gold ring that matched the one hanging from a silver chain around Autumn's neck.

"Mom?"

"Autumn."

"Mom?" Autumn wheezed. Her head was spinning. How could the deceased mother she longed for be here in the same room with her now?

"How? How are you alive? Why are you here?"

"Autumn, I know you have questions and I want to explain everything to you. Come and sit down."

Autumn obeyed and took a seat on the floral couch next to her mother.

"All I wanted was for you to be safe. Everything that we did was to keep you safe."

"Safe from what?"

"From the zakari. They are dark powerful beings who want to either end our line or convert us to their darkness."

"Jack mentioned them," Autumn said, looking in Jack's direction. She had nearly forgotten he was in the room, but she wanted him close to her. The look on his face caused Autumn's gut to clench. He wasn't looking back *at* her, he looked *through* her like a stranger in a shopping mall.

"Please excuse me, Your Highness. Princess," he said bowing to both women before heading out the front door.

"Princess?" Autumn repeated. When it rained it poured.

"Yes, Autumn," her mother said as if reading her thoughts.

CHAPTER THIRTEEN

"You are a princess of the bakazi. You will be queen someday," Rayvn said, rising from the couch and pacing toward the kitchen.

"Why didn't you come back for me, Mom?" Autumn's head was spinning. She sat on the couch with arms crossed around her waist. How was she supposed to feel? The mother she longed for had been sitting on a magic throne for over a decade without so much as a postcard to let Autumn know she was still breathing.

"I know you're upset but let me explain," Rayvn said, taking a seat at the bar. Probably a good idea to give her some space right now.

"I left the safety of the mansion before you were born. I couldn't risk anyone finding out about you. I had to run to keep us both alive."

Rayvn's eyes pled for understanding.

"Let me start from the beginning. My parents kept me sheltered but I was a curious young lady. The more they tried to keep me under lock and key the more I tried to discover the so-called dangers of the world. I found the danger my parents warned me about twenty-six years ago outside a club in Austin. I also found love. Your father. We were not supposed to be together but the feelings between us were like a fire meeting a tornado. I wanted to be with him more than anything in the world, but I had a responsibility to my family and my people. I was to be the next queen of the bakazi and Mikael was... is... a zakari. He and I knew what would happen if our relationship was discovered."

"What would have happened?" Autumn snapped. "Jack told me it's forbidden to... be with zakari and their offspring but he never explained the consequences."

"The parents and the child can either be exiled or put to death. Rayvn shuttered. I would never uphold such a law today, Autumn. I need you to know that."

Autumn sighed and uncrossed her arms. Her hand closed around the gold ring on the silver chain that hung around her neck, a nervous habit she'd been indulging in more in the past few days.

"Neither of us realized I was pregnant when things ended between us. When I found out, I hid my pregnancy for months not knowing what I would do when you were born."

"So, I'm like Jack? I'm a spawn?"

"Yes, sweet girl. I gave birth to you a few weeks after leaving my family home. A friend, a witch, helped me change my appearance and I ran with you as soon as I could. I disappeared hoping that everyone would think I had been kidnapped or killed. My plan worked for a while but, you came into your powers faster than I anticipated. I think that was due to your zakari side. Bakazi don't come into their powers until age twenty-two after their transition. But by eleven years old you were causing windstorms without realizing it. New powers are like a beacon in the magic community. I reached out to my friend again, and he helped me hide you and bind your powers.

I knew the spell wouldn't last forever. Your bakazi transition to adulthood was inevitable. I just thought I had more time to prepare you, but it was already too late. They came for us."

"Is that what happened the night you…died?"

"Yes. They came to our home. We had just come back from a trip to the grocery store. I felt them as soon as we pulled into the driveway. My parents never stopped looking for me, but they are not the ones who found us. I backed out and tried to drive away but they followed. They chased us down and ran us off the road as we crossed the bridge. When we went into the water, my only concern was you. I took off my ring and put it in your hand. That ring," Rayvn said, nodding toward the gold ring on the silver chain that had hung from Autumn's neck for years.

"I don't know how Vervina had her premonition of you if you still wear it." Rayvn frowned.

"That ring is spelled to hide magic. My friend spelled it with his family's grimoire. He would have never overridden the spell. That's why I gave it to you. I wanted you to be protected, even after the binding spell wore off. I reached into your mind and told you to go and hide until morning."

"I hid and waited for you in the forest all night. I could hear you in my head for a while and then everything stopped," Autumn said. Recalling that night.

"I said the prayer you taught me over and over again until I fell asleep."

"It was a spell. I wanted you to be able to call to the witch whose magic hid you in case you ever needed help."

"I held the saams off for as long as I could. One of them overpowered me and ended up with his hands around my throat. I blacked out and when I woke up, I was back at the mansion. My parents rescued me. When I removed my ring, they found me. I'm so sorry sweet girl. I'm so sorry."

Rayvn rose from the bar stool and took a step in Autumn's direction with one arm outstretched toward her daughter.

Autumn was trying to find understanding and started to reach toward her mother when the world exploded around them. All chaos and smoke.

The wind started to blow like a tornado formed in the midst of all the mayhem.

A blazing hole opened up through the kitchen wall. The ferocious wind caused the fire to spread easily.

Autumn squinted through the smoke looking for her mother. The mother she lost as a child was back and Autumn could not lose her now.

"Mom!"

She could barely hear her own screams over the howling wind. When no answer came, she ventured toward the burning kitchen to where her mom had been standing a moment ago.

Autumn shrieked as a fireball sizzled across her shoulder.

Big arms wrapped around Autumn's waist and pulled her to the floor.

CHAPTER THIRTEEN

"We have to fly," Jack said close to her ear.

"No. My mom—"

"Lucky has her. They're gone. She's safe. We have to go."

Autumn nodded and tucked her body in close to Jack. She remembered to take a deep breath and the next minute she was laying on the grass in front of a large barn.

"Who was that at the cottage? Was that a saam?"

"Yes. The fucking worst kind," Jack said raising to his feet and reaching for Autumn.

"What kind?"

"Enforcer. Fucking pit bulls for crossroads deals. When a human or magical being makes a crossroads deal enforcers do the soul collecting. They will not stop coming for you."

Autumn joined Jack on the vertical.

"But I haven't made any crossroads deal. I didn't even know that was a real thing."

"They have been known to take a side job for a fee. Someone ordered a hit. Jack explained while ushering Autumn inside the large barn-dominium. We have to find that person and kill them to break the contract."

Jack said *we* but what he meant was *he* would find the fuck wad who order a hit on Autumn and introduce him to hell. When the motherfucker was well acquainted with the hell on earth that Jack would manufacture, that piece of shit would beg for death.

"Jack you're snarling," Autumn started to back away.

"Not at you. Come on let's take a look at that arm."

Autumn looked at her left shoulder. The sleeve hung loose only held on by the under-arm stitching. She had been hit with a fireball. The skin still felt hot and was already blistering. "It's fine. I want to see my mom," she said.

"Lucky probably took her to the big house. Let me get you some pants and I will take you to her. Sage should have something that will fit you."

Autumn looked down at her bare feet. She was only wearing Jack's t-shirt. The one he had demanded she remove last night. When she'd woken up to voices at the cottage she hadn't bothered with pants or anything else.

"Okay," Autumn said.

Chapter Fourteen

The mansion was grand and oversized. Autumn felt out of place looking down at her borrowed clothes and socks. The basketball shorts fit a little tighter than she liked but at least her ass was covered. As for footwear Sage's socks were the only thing she could squeeze into, and the floor felt cool under her near-naked feet. The dark tile in the front entryway was speckled with a vibrant blue stone. It reminded Autumn of the blue glow from the dream she'd had about falling into the river. All of her dreams were connected to this place. To this life that was now her new reality.

After they reached the second-story landing, they walked past a large open space lined with bookcases. The mid-morning sun shone through a large window with bench seating that broke up what would have been wall-to-wall shelves. Past the library, they entered a hallway with a set of double doors on each side. A man with long locs stood outside the double doors on the left. The guy was dressed in black cargo pants and the biggest Jem and the Holograms shirt she had ever seen. He was taller than Jack but not as broad. All the myths that she had read said faeries were small, winged human-like creatures who lived in mushroom villages. None of these guys were even small enough for a compact car let alone a mushroom village.

"Hey, Lucky. How is she?" Jack asked.

"A healer is tending to Queen Rayvn. You can go in if you'd like, Princess."

Autumn opened her mouth in surprise and looked at Jack.

"I stopped by the cottage this morning to bring a few supplies for you two. I was on the porch with Jack before the attack. He told me you're our queen's daughter."

"Autumn," she said as she started toward the double doors. "My name is Autumn."

Once Autumn disappeared into the queen's private room, Lucky turned to Jack.

"She is beautiful like her mother. Does she know she's bound to you?"

"She is not. Not anymore."

Lucky was the most intuitive of them all. He could especially sense a sexual prospect as soon as they stepped into the same room. Lucky's libido radar could tell that both Jack and Autumn had been claimed. Bonded.

"A bond cannot be broken, Jack. You know that. That is unless you plan to kill her or let that enforcer get at her."

"I know how a bond works."

"Then you are going to tell her?"

"How is our queen?" Jack asked, attempting the change the subject.

"The *tari* says the queen's injuries are severe. It will take more than one attempt to revive her. She has some concussive injuries from the explosion, including internal bleeding. I wish I could have gotten to her sooner. The healer will stay at the queen's bedside tonight. I will take guard duty."

"Where is Carver?"

"He had some other business. That's why he sent me to make the supply delivery to you. He might have finally caught a lead in his brother's case."

"His brother's case will have to wait. We need to identify the person who hired that enforcer. How did that asshole find us?"

"I don't know but Autumn and Queen Rayvn are safe for now. No one without bakazi blood is getting past that blue stone border out front."

Jack knew Lucky was right. The llanite border had stood as protection for the royal family for hundreds of years. It ran under the ground and surrounded the royal homestead. It was not by accident that the bakazi settled in the Hill Country. Llanite could only be found in the Hill Country. The blue rock called to them. Magic to magic.

"No one leaves the grounds for now. We'll all be safer here. That asshole knows we have Autumn. His next step will be to look for one of us to torture or trade for her location. Have you seen Sage?"

"She said something about a hair appointment this morning."

"Damn it. You stay here. I'll call her and Carver back to the mansion and we'll meet later to figure this out."

Rayvn's body lay still under the quilt on the king-sized bed. A blue light glowed on her chest. Autumn watched for the rise and fall there that would signal life.

"She is resting."

Autumn turned to see a masculine figure in dress pants and a button-down emerging from a door that must be her mother's bathroom. His sleeves were rolled up exposing intricate tattoos on both forearms.

"I am Hamilton. I am a *tari*."

The guy looked like a quarterback.

"Tari," Autumn repeated. "That's a healer, right?"

"Yes, I am a healer."

"Then why is she still unconscious? I know I'm new to all this magic stuff but if you're a healer why haven't you healed her?"

"I can only do what the universe allows. I know that sounds very hippie-dippie spiritual but that's how bakazi magic works.

CHAPTER FOURTEEN

We are connected to the universe. The queen sustained serious injuries. I was able to stabilize her, and I will sit with her tonight in case of an emergency."

"You mean like if her heart stops?" Autumn snapped.

She was a bit surprised at the panic in her voice. She just didn't want to lose her mom again.

"Shouldn't she be in a hospital? How will you even know if she's having a medical emergency? She's not on any monitors," Autumn tried to sound calmer.

"The blue-speckled rock there," Hamilton said, gesturing to her mother's chest.

It looked similar to the tile in the entryway.

"It's tuned to her body and should help with her body's natural healing. As long as it glows her heart remains strong. If the stone stops glowing that means the queen is in crisis."

"Can she hear my voice? Do you think she knows I'm with her?" Autumn asked.

"The blue stone started to glow brighter when you walked into the room. The queen has strong feelings about you just being near her."

"I'm Autumn. I'm her daughter."

"Daughter?" A range of emotions crossed Hamilton's face. First shock then acceptance and finally pure joy.

"Well, welcome home," he said with a genuine smile. "May I heal you, Princess?"

"It's Autumn and yes, please. My arm is really throbbing."

Hamilton rubbed his hands together until a white light appeared between his palms. When he placed his hands on Autumn's wounded shoulder, they felt warm. It was like relaxing in a hot bath. And just like that the throbbing pain was gone.

"Thank you, Hamilton," Autumn said.

"It was my pleasure, Princess Autumn," he said with a smile.

Autumn left her mother's room confident that Hamilton would keep a watchful eye. Plus, Lucky stood like a sentry at her mom's door. The queen was safe, but someone had tried to murder Autumn and almost succeeded in killing her mother. She needed to find Jack and figure out how to keep herself and those she loved alive. Jack's voice was a welcome clue to his location. Autumn walked down the stairs following the sound.

"I don't care if your braids aren't finished. You get your ass back to Base now Sage, or so help me I will send Lucky to get you," Jack said before disconnecting his call.

Autumn walked toward Jack with her arms open.

Jack pulled her into his arms. His brain said it was a bad idea, but the bond was still in place. Her sorrow was his own. He would do literally anything to take away her pain.

"What are we going to do?" Autumn asked.

CHAPTER FOURTEEN

She looked so lost.

"It's going to be alright. I've called the squad back to Base. This property is protected. Everyone will be safe here while we figure out who's after you."

"Kamara! What if the enforcer goes to my house and finds Kamara there? He'll kill her. I have to—"

"Kamara is safe. Carver is bringing her here with him."

"Carver's bringing her here?"

"Yeah."

"Thank goodness," Autumn said, relaxing in his arms.

Her soft curves felt too good against his body. He wanted this to be his forever, but their forbidden bond could not stand. It had to be broken with death and he would be the one to accept that penalty. But he would hold on to the feel of her body against his until he took his last breath.

"Autumn West?" said a tall thin man as he walked into the living room. He had a smile on his face, but no joy in his words.

Jack dropped his arms and took a step away from Autumn. This would not go well.

"Your Highness," Jack said in greeting.

"Orphan," Silas said, returning Jack's greeting without taking his eyes off Autumn.

"I am King Silas, husband of the departed Queen Olive and father of Queen Rayvn. You look very much like your mother."

"Have we met before?" Autumn asked.

"No child I would remember meeting you. I do not doubt that. My daughter only mentioned that she was seeking a wayward named Autumn West. Now seeing you in person I recognize the features of the women I love. You have your mother's eyes and your grandmother's nose."

Silas's fake smile faded as he turned to Jack.

"Does the queen know what you are trying to do, orphan?"

"Your Highness. I am sure that I do not understand."

Jack didn't like the air the dowager king was giving off. The dislike of the kin squad was nothing new, but Silas seemed to be taunting Autumn.

"I am the one who is having trouble understanding. I know that my power is not what it once was, but I do remember our laws even as others do not," said Silas.

"I am aware of the laws, Your Highness," Jack replied, clenching and unclenching his hands. He could feel the burn in his chest. Silas was needling him with the fact that any physical relationship with a bakazi was forbidden. But the feel of Autumn's body wrapped around his was too fresh in his mind. Jack had the urge to snap Silas's neck and disappear with his woman, but he could not lose control here. The dowager king was right. The princess could never be his.

Autumn watched the exchange as if it were a Ping-Pong match. Her head moved from side to side with each response.

"Hi," Autumn said, waving her hands between the men.

"Kinda new to all the faerie- uh bakazi royal family stuff. Are there some rules or sacred laws that I should be made aware of? Do I need a chaperone to be with my friend?"

CHAPTER FOURTEEN

"This is not your friend, Autumn. He needs to be reminded of his status and you need to be made aware of the rules of your station. There is to be no mixing of the bloodlines. You are not to fraternize with those below your station. Especially his kind," said Silas, looking down his nose at his granddaughter.

Autumn looked at Jack as if she expected a fight to break out at any moment. Instead, Jack stood still and quiet with his head bowed as tradition commanded. He needed some peace and quiet for just a few minutes to get his zakari side under control. Maybe Autumn would understand what he had to do now. A bond could only be broken by death, and he would not let Autumn's heart be the one to stop beating. She was innocent in this. She didn't know the consequences of a bond with him. He did the crime. He would pay the cost.

"You are excused, orphan. Go back to your quarters."

Jack began to move toward the door.

"Are you for real?" said Autumn.

"This is very real, Princess," Silas answered.

"Jack, wait!" she called.

Jack kept moving as if his name had changed.

"Jack! I know you hear me. Stop. Please. Talk to me."

Jack stopped at the doorway to look over his shoulder. His eyes still not meeting Autumn's.

"What is it, Princess?" he asked, unable to control his rough tone.

"Why did you let him treat you like that?"

"He is your grandfather and part of the royal family. As are you. I should have never overstepped with you."

"Overstepped? You mean you regret what happened last night."

Jack pressed his lips together, holding back the truth of how he felt. He had to end this conversation. If anyone overheard the fact that they had slept together the information would be fatal. He could not let anything happen to Autumn because of him.

"I have to go. I'm sorry."

Chapter Fifteen

Angry tears crept down her cheeks as Autumn stormed up the stairs. She would not look back no matter how much it hurt. *Don't look back. Don't look back. Do not look back.* Repeating the words like a mantra in her head was necessary to keep her dignity. Her first instinct was to fight. She needed to fight *with* him in order to fight *for* them. But why fight for someone who didn't want her? Jack didn't want to be around her? He regretted sleeping with her? Well it was his loss. So why did her chest feel like it had been ripped open with a plastic butter knife? Why could she not control her emotions when that fucking faerie was anywhere near her?

I belong to you.

She had wanted his words to mean so much more. Is this how Kamara felt about Carver? She had been catching feelings and he just wanted to check her off his to do list. *Bastard!*

A strong wind blew through the second-floor hallway. Autumn turned to find the source of the breeze but as she rotated so did the wind. The air swirled around her, ruffling her curls.

"Autumn. Are you okay?"

The wind immediately stopped.

"Carver. Is Kamara here with you?" Autumn asked.

"Yeah. Just got here. Flying didn't agree with her," he said, rubbing his flat belly. "Upset stomach. She's at Base."

"Thank goodness she's safe. I'm glad she's here. I need to talk to her."

"Maybe we should get your emotions under control before you see Kamara. Looks like your powers are growing and somebody must have pissed you off."

"Powers?"

"The wind. That was you, Autumn. When we lose control of our emotions, we lose control of our powers, too."

"I — I don't know how I did that. I'm not very good at this whole magic being thing."

"So who pissed you off?"

Autumn grabbed the gold ring on the silver chain that hung around her neck and shuffled her feet.

"Jack," he said with a matter-of-fact tone.

Autumn's gaze snapped to Carver's face. "I don't want to talk to you about Jack."

"It's alright." Carver raised his hands in surrender. "Coming into your powers is a tough time, especially for a wayward. When did you transition?"

"I haven't yet," answered Autumn.

"Strange," Carver said. "You must be getting close. I would be glad to show you a few things, but I'm supposed to relieve Lucky for a few hours. What has Jack– I mean... uh, what have you learned so far?"

A breeze ruffled Autumn's coils. After a few deep breaths in through the nose and out through the mouth Autumn answered the question.

"Jack showed me his powers, but I guess we haven't had time to work on my own."

"Come on," Carver said, walking toward Lucky's post.

Lucky was still standing in the hall outside her mother's bedroom.

"Hey, Lucky. Jack wants me to relieve you."

"Why? I told him I would take the first watch. It's been less than an hour."

"I think you may have to do a fly-by on Sage. She's refusing to leave her hair appointment."

"Damn it. Excuse my language, Princess," Lucky said.

"Princess?" Carver asked, looking at Autumn with wide eyes.

"Haven't you heard? Autumn is Queen Rayvn's daughter," Lucky said with a wide smile, taking entirely too much pleasure in dropping the princess bomb before leaving to deal with Sage.

"Please don't start acting weird. I'm just Autumn West, wayward fae and you were going to help me with my magic."

"Alright," Carver agreed after a long moment. "I can't show you all the elements inside the mansion. We don't want to destroy the place, but I can show you the wind and water. Do you know what your passive power is?"

"I'm a *siliana*."

"Cool," Carver said.

Autumn watched as Carver held one hand palm side up between them until blue sparks swirled up from his palm to form a sphere.

"Is that water?" asked Autumn.

"Yep. You bakazi pure breeds can control the elements but spawn can conjure them." he smiled. "We'll practice water manipulation first. You can use this same technique to control your telepathy. Look at the water and in mind tell it what to do."

Autumn didn't correct his assumption that she was pure bakazi. She wasn't ready to explain her zakari side.

"Do I need to wave my hands around or point to it or something?" she asked.

"Your hands might help at first. It's a mental thing. When you get more comfortable you won't need hand motions. I want you to pull the water out of my hand."

Autumn eyed the sphere with uncertainty but held out her hand. She squinted at the water, commanding it to come to her. The ball of water stretched and flattened slightly then moved toward Autumn. She kept up her concentration until the liquid tickled the palm of her hand and formed a lop-sided sphere.

Autumn gasped.

"I did it," she said in disbelief.

"Yes!" Carver cheered just before the water Autumn had been controlling splashed to the floor.

Autumn worked on taming her powers for about an hour before a loud grumbling noise started to come from her stomach.

"Who knew that learning to control magical powers would work up such an appetite?" she said.

"Why do you think we eat so much?" Carter laughed. "I'm sure Jack can cook something at the house for you and Kamara."

Jack didn't want to see her tonight. Maybe ever after the way he reacted to dear old Grandpa. Come to think of it, Jack had been doing nothing but trying to get rid of her the whole time they were together. Maybe it was a pity fuck.

"Thanks for the offer, Carver but I'm really tired. I think I'll find something to eat here. Do you think Kamara will stop by later?"

"Yeah, she wanted to come straight here, but I asked her to wait until she feels better. When I see her, I'll send her your way."

"Thanks. I'm on the other end of the hall."

"Hey if you want a quick snack there's always fruit in the kitchen downstairs. Make a U-turn at the bottom of the stairs. You can't miss it."

Autumn found the kitchen. Of course, she couldn't miss it. It was huge. Kamara would love the white stone island. She always complained that their kitchen didn't have enough counter space to spread out. This island would probably seat eight people. On the counter behind the island, Autumn spotted a bowl of fruit and her stomach let out a loud rumble. An apple would have to be her dinner for tonight. Practicing magic was a workout but she had to admit it was fun and Carver said she would be stronger and more in control after her transition.

After washing her zero-calorie dinner under the kitchen faucet she took a bite not bothering to dry the fruit. This had to be her mother's touch. When she was a kid her mom had always made sure there were healthy snacks for Autumn to grab on the go. The memory made her smile as she headed for the stairs.

When she reached her bedroom door most of the apple was gone. Maybe she should have grabbed a banana too but there was no way she was trekking back to the kitchen.

Once she got inside, she noticed that someone had laid a satin pajama set and robe on her bed.

"Nice," she sighed.

She headed to the adjoining bathroom to shower and change. She had been so worried about her mom before that she'd barely had time to change clothes.

Autumn turned the knob to start the water. The warm spray felt like heaven on her skin. Not surprisingly there was shampoo, conditioner, and citrus-scented body wash in the shower cubby. Normally she wouldn't dare wash her hair away from home, but her coils smelled like smoke thanks to that asshole at the cottage. Nothing was normal about the last forty-eight hours, so she lathered up.

Thirty minutes later Autumn stepped out of the shower. She wrapped one soft white towel around her body and another around her hair. It would take hours to dry but she was too tired to search for a blow dryer.

The clock on the nightstand read 7:22PM There was a small bowl of berries on the nightstand by the bed. How had she missed that before getting in the shower?

"I must be really tired," she said, grabbing a couple of blueberries and popping them in her mouth. When she sank her teeth into the healthy snack her mouth was flooded with a bitter-tasting juice. She scrunched up her face and squeezed her eyes shut at the tart taste. Her stomach cramped at the introduction of the bitter fruit. The pain started small but grew like a wave. She needed to sit down. She tried to breathe through the pain. Thankfully after a few minutes, the cramping stopped, and her body relaxed.

Autumn opened her eyes and looked around. What was wrong with those berries? She had been in so much pain that she didn't even remember laying on the bed. She sat up to stretch and that's when she saw it.

A person was lying on the floor near the foot of the bed.

"Hey, are you okay?" She lowered her feet to the floor and approached what seemed to be a lifeless body.

"Oh shit."

The body on the ground was her.

Lucky walked into the house to the rhythmic thumping of someone hitting the heavy bag and he could guess who it might be.

He headed straight for the gym in the back room of the house. Jack was covered in sweat. Fists and feet flew at the heavy bag with no signs of slowing. The temperature of the room was at least twenty degrees higher than the rest of the house. Jack was pissed. He didn't acknowledge Lucky's presence.

Lucky positioned himself behind the object of Jack's fury. A dangerous position for sure but his friend needed to have a conversation.

"Jack," Lucky said, peering at his friend while holding the heavy bag still.

"Move," Jack snapped.

"Jack, we need to talk."

"Move."

Jack's eyes were glowing. His emotions were out of control, but this conversation needed to happen now.

"Fine, I'll talk while you continue to throw a fit."

"Fuck you."

"You need to talk to Autumn."

"Fuck off, Lucky. I need you to find Sage. I don't need to have a Dr. Phil moment."

"Did I hear my name?" Sage chose that moment to make her appearance sporting a fresh set of pink and black box braids.

"Where the hell have you been, Sage? I called you almost an hour ago."

"I told Rapunzel with dreads over there I couldn't leave in the middle of my appointment," she said, pointing at Lucky.

"I'm here now though. Where's the fire?" Sage asked.

"First, I told you to stop calling me Rapunzel. I'm more Elsa to your Anna," Lucky replied.

Sage shared some sign language, but Lucky was unbothered.

"Second, I told you I would brief you after I talk to Jack. You never listen," Lucky continued.

"You can brief her now. Somewhere else. Not here," Jack volunteered.

"Give me fifteen minutes, Sage," Lucky said.

"Yes, sir," Sage responded with a grin before going to do as she was asked.

"Get the fuck out, Lucky."

"She can't help who her parents are, Jack. We should know that. I know what the laws say but Autumn is a wayward. She doesn't know our laws. Did you explain things to her before you bonded with her? Maybe there is a way—"

"She's the princess!" Jack shouted, striking out at the punching bag. Lucky was knocked to the ground by the explosive force and the bag was on fire. Flames were spreading from the spot on the bag where Jack had connected the punch. The blaze crawled up his arms and danced across his chest.

Jack's growl rattled the windows until Lucky was afraid they might shatter.

Lucky rose to his full height and stretched his arms wide. In a practice motion, he brought his arms together in front of his body, gathering air along the way. In a rush, Lucky pushed the air at Jack's fire-wrapped body. It was like blowing out a big pissed-off birthday candle. Lucky hammered his friend with the wind until it was Jack's turn to fall to the floor.

Jack lay on his back with his eyes closed, chest pumping up and down from the exertion.

"Are you trying to kill us all or just yourself? Listen to me," Lucky said, reaching down to grab Jack's hand and haul him to his feet. "Autumn is a beautiful, powerful woman. If she is anything like her mother, she will make a great queen one day and nothing is stopping you from being by her side."

"You stay away from Autumn. She is not one of your club sluts," Jack ground out.

"Damn, bro. No one is trying to take her away from you, Jack. Do you think I would do that shit? I'm not as much of a fuck boy as you all think. Autumn is yours," Lucky said.

"The zakari inside me wants her. It wants to possess her. Mark her like an animal. That's the darkness within me. My rapist father fucked any chance to have a normal life or a family. This is why the law is in place. I have already made the mistake of letting things get out of hand. I have to end it now before it's too late. Even if it means ending my own life to break the bond."

"You've bonded to her. That's not a zakari thing. That's a bakazi thing. Jack, the law is in place to keep our zakari DNA out of the bakazi gene pool but that may not apply to Autumn."

"What do you mean? She is a bakazi princess. The law *especially* applies to her."

"Why was Autumn's birth kept secret? We know her mother is bakazi, but what do we know about her father?" Lucky asked.

"What are—"

Jack froze like someone pressed the pause button on his life.

"Jack?" Lucky waved his hand in front of Jack's suddenly vacant stare. Jack's body was still standing in the gym, but his mind had been forced somewhere else.

Chapter Sixteen

Stay calm. Autumn told herself. She closed her eyes and took several deep breaths in through the nose, out through the mouth.

Wake up.

Wake up.

Another set of deep breaths.

Wake up.

Wake up!

"Why can't I wake up?" Autumn groaned.

She looked down at her body and tried to remember what happened. The last thing she remembered was getting out of the shower.

Her body was still wrapped in a white towel. She needed to figure out what happened after her shower.

CHAPTER SIXTEEN

There was a two-piece pajama set and a robe lying on the bed. Someone had put them there before she made her way to her room.

Autumn scanned the room for any sign of a fight. If someone else had been involved she would have thrown hands. No broken windows, no overturned chairs, no busted light fixtures. Nothing was out of the ordinary except for a bowl of fruit that seemed to have fallen off the nightstand.

"Blueberries," she whispered to herself.

She had eaten an apple but was still hungry when she got out of the shower. She'd found the berries on the nightstand and had eaten a few of the blueberries, but they were bitter. Were they really blueberries?

"Did someone poison me? Am I dead? I ate weird poison berries and now I'm...dead. I can't be dead. I just found this whole new life."

Autumn had so much to live for. Her mom was back. She had magic powers. She was exploring new relationships. Jack...

"No, if I were dead, I would be floating away from my body or there would be a bright light or something. Right?" Autumn asked herself out loud.

She looked closely at her body this time. She had to be alive. Her back moved up and down. She was breathing but she couldn't just sit around and wait to be found. She didn't know how much longer her body could fight whatever she had ingested.

If she was only unconscious and not dead, she should be able to use her telepathy to dream walk.

She had already seen how strong her connection was to Jack. No matter how he felt about her this was literally life or death.

Autumn closed her eyes and pictured his face. He was talking to someone.

"You've bonded to her. That's not a zakari thing. That's a bakazi thing," the person was saying.

"Jack."

"Jack, it's Autumn. I need you."

She could hear him, but she couldn't see him like she did before. The connection was not as strong as it had been the last time she entered his thoughts.

"Autumn?" Jack responded.

"Yes. I need your help. I'm at the mansion in my room. My body is on the floor. I can't wake up. I think I'm... I'm dying."

It was taking so much strength to communicate.

"What?"

"I think someone poisoned me, Jack. Please help me. I'm so tired."

"Hang on. I'm on my way."

Autumn hoped Jack would be there fast enough to keep her from floating away from her body permanently. She wasn't ready to die. She didn't want to let go.

CHAPTER SIXTEEN

Jack blinked his eyes as his awareness returned. Lucky stood in front of him with a concerned look on his face.

"Autumn. It was Autumn. She's *siliana*."

"She was in your mind?" Lucky asked.

Jack could feel the fire growing in his chest. The zakari within raged and clawed to be set free. His vision flashed blue and for a moment Jack wanted to let the monster out of its cage. He wanted the universe to burn for allowing this to happen.

"Someone poisoned her. We have to get to her now," Jack growled, bolting out of the gym.

Jack ran through the house with Lucky close behind. All he could do was picture Autumn's lifeless body on the floor. He should have never left her alone. Fuck the rules. He belonged with her. He belonged *to* her.

"What's going on?" Kamara asked as both men ran past her on the front porch.

"Autumn's hurt," Lucky replied when Jack simply snarled and kept running.

"I'm coming with you," Kamara said.

They all sprinted across the lawn. When they arrived at the front entrance of the mansion Jack and Lucky stood side by side in front of the grand wooden door. Jack wanted to run through the damn thing like a tank. Instead, he conjured a fireball big enough to blow it off the hinges.

"Jack! No." Lucky yelled. "We don't want to hurt any innocent people on the other side of that door."

But that's where his friend was wrong. He wanted to destroy something and in that moment Jack didn't care what happened to anyone else. He would burn the world as long as it meant getting to Autumn.

Lucky entered the security code on the keypad next to the door with one hand while sending a gust of wind toward Jack.

Jack bared his fangs in protest but refocused once the door was open. He took the stairs two at a time. Autumn could be dying, and she was scared and all alone. Why didn't he stay by her side?

Jack went left when he reached the landing and ran to Autumn's door.

The scene inside was like a nightmare. Autumn was lying face down on the floor and didn't appear to be breathing.

"No, no, no, no, no," Jack said as he dropped to his knees and scooped Autumn's limp body into his arms. Her wet hair clung to her face.

"Autumn wake up baby," he pleaded, shaking her in his arms.

"Lucky get help!" Jack yelled.

"I can help her," Kamara said, sinking to her knees in front of Jack. "Lay her down flat on the floor."

Jack felt helpless as he watched his Autumn slip away forever. There was nothing he could do. The darkness inside him stirred again but what could that side of him do to help in this moment? He would fight anyone or kill anything for this woman, but he was useless in this moment.

Kamara was saying something. She loved Autumn too. Did she feel like there were knives in her chest? Did Kamara feel like there was a vice around her throat? Is that what she was saying?

"I heard yelling. What's going on?" said Carver as he walked in on the scene in Autumn's bedroom.

Kamara's eyes darted toward the doorway for only a second.

"Someone poisoned the princess," Lucky explained.

"Shit."

"Lay her down, Jack. I can help her," Kamara repeated, finally getting through to him.

Jack gently placed Autumn's body on the floor, making sure to hold his hand under her head until she was lying flat.

Kamara started to rub her hands together above Autumn's body. White light appeared between her fingers and spread to cover both hands completely.

"What is she doing?" Lucky asked.

Kamara laid one glowing hand on Autumn's belly and another on her neck.

"She's a *tari*," said Carver.

The room fell silent. After a few minutes, Kamara started to speak softly. She was whispering something to the universe that was between her and the creator. The glow in Kamara's hands started to spread all over Autumn's body until she was wrapped in a cocoon of white light so bright that everyone needed to shield their eyes. The hairs on the back of Jack's neck stood up. His body tingled as the light started to radiate outward from Autumn's position. He could feel it washing over him as well. The energy pouring from that light was like a sustained low-voltage electrocution. Kamara's whispered chants mixed with the buzzing of the powerful energy surrounding Autumn and permeating the room.

Jack had never witnessed a healing like this. He prayed it would work. Life would be agony without her. If she died, he would follow her to the afterlife and beg her to accept him there.

A gasp came from somewhere inside the light as it started to dim. Autumn was firmly back in the land of the living.

An unfamiliar tingle started behind Jack's eyes seemingly in response to Autumn's reanimation. His chest burned but not in anger. This was something else. He could see Kamara helping Autumn sit up but the scene was wavy like he was watching them through water. Then he felt the moisture on his face and the burning in his chest started to ease. This is what it felt like to let go. He could never change the person he was or the one he belonged to.

"Thank the universe," Jack said as he pulled Autumn into his arms.

"I should have never left you alone," he said.

"Promise you won't do it again," said Autumn, wiping away his tears.

"I belong to you. I will never leave you. And I will find the corpse who did this and put him in the ground."

Grunts of approval came from the doorway. Carver and Lucky were standing there and looked like two concerned parents. But they weren't looking at Autumn.

"Are you sure you're alright?" asked a quiet voice behind her.

"Kam?" Autumn said, twisting to see her best friend. "I'm so glad you're here. Are you okay? You look exhausted. What happened?"

"We'll talk later," Kamara said, grabbing onto the bed to haul herself off the floor. "I think your man wants some time alone with you."

Once everyone had cleared out and the door was locked, Autumn sat on the bed. Jack couldn't stop thinking about her lifeless body lying on the floor. What if she hadn't been able to reach him telepathically?

"Jack. Come sit with me."

The mattress dipped as Jack sat beside her. His nylon joggers rubbed against her naked thigh and his body responded.

"I was trying to protect you. Our laws are very strict. My kind is not allowed to bond with your kind, Autumn and that's what happened between us. It wasn't just sex. That's why we felt the pull."

"The pull? What does that mean?"

"The tingling feeling we get when we're close to each other. The jolt we feel when we touch. The magnetism between us. It's called the pull because that's what it feels like. We are being pulled toward our destined mates."

He pushed her away to save her and it nearly cost him everything. She could have died thinking he regretted being with her. *Fuck that.*

"I bonded with you. That means I will never want another. I will only have a family with you. The law was written as part of the royal family's plan to let us live and serve as the royal guard. They did not want to risk zakari DNA mixing with the bakazi bloodline. No more children like the kin squad could ever be born. We were watched closely growing up. The royals thought we would be too dangerous and unstable. That's why the penalty for producing a spawn is death."

"I know. My mother told me everything at the cottage."

"I have been loyal to my queen but if she would stand against us or try to harm you..."

"She won't. After you left the room, she told me who my father is. He's a zakari. They fell in love. I think she still loves him. Anyway, she said she would never uphold a law that makes a similar relationship punishable."

"I will not leave you again, Autumn."

"Good." Autumn sighed leaning her head on Jack's shoulder.

"I don't care about some stupid law, Jack. If you want to be with me, I want to be with you. Besides, if my father is a zakari, that makes us the same."

"Not exactly, *Kipeyo*. You are a princess of the bakazi. Queen Rayvn has no other heir. You will inherit the throne and some bakazi will object. I have heard stories of it happening before, but I will protect you. They are free to live with their objections or die if their objections become actions."

Jack turned to meet Autumn's big brown eyes. He needed her to believe him. To look into his soul and know that he meant every word.

"You are mine, Autumn West. The master of my heart. I belong to you."

Autumn nodded slightly before pressing a delicate finger against Jack's lips.

"No more words, Jack. If I'm yours, show me now. I need to feel it," Autumn whispered.

Jack's hand trailed up her neck to rest on her jaw, sending shivers of pleasure through her body. He used his grip to guide her closer and their lips met in a heated kiss, their tongues exploring each other's mouths.

Jack's hands moved, catching the top of the towel still wrapped around her body. He wasted no time caressing her exposed flesh. He loved the way she responded to him. Arching into his touch and filling his hands with her soft curves.

How could he have been so stupid to think about giving her up? She was everything. The promise of a life he hoped for. Without this woman life was empty.

Jack pushed Autumn onto the fluffy comforter and started to kiss his way down her body stopping to linger at her breast. He pulled her nipple into his mouth flicking it with his tongue and enjoying Autumn's sharp inhale. He moaned his approval before releasing the hard tip to continue his exploration.

He had nearly lost everything.

Autumn moaned as his fingers found her sex, rubbing her clit.

She moved her hips against Jack's hand, begging him to enter her.

"Please, Jack." Her hands moved to his waistband, pulling in urgency. Jack's erection pushed at the nylon fabric, and Autumn smiled when she freed his shaft.

"I want you inside me."

Jack's blue eyes glowed as he shoved his pants free.

"Whatever you want *Kipeyo* but first..."

Autumn's body jerked as he ran his finger over her sensitive clit and pushed into her wet core.

Then lifting the moisture-soaked digit to his lips, he closed his eyes and took his finger into his mouth. She tasted like honey-covered strawberries. The sweetest thing he could ever know, and she was his forever. When Jack opened his eyes, he knew they resembled shattered glass. He could see the blue glow illuminating Autumn's skin.

Autumn lowered her gaze to the spot where they would be joined. His wayward wanted to watch them become one and he wanted to make it good for her. Jack wrapped his hand around his shaft pumping his fist up and down before making his next move. He swiped the thick head along Autumn's wetness, rubbing up and down until she started to squirm. Then Jack used his wet cock to paint the letter J on her mound. Autumn smirked and bit her bottom lip just before he covered her mouth with his own. He thrust his tongue into her mouth, claiming it. She lifted her hips to align with him and he slammed his erection into her. Groaning as her muscles rippled around his shaft.

"Damnit!" he muttered as he pulled back until only the head of his shaft remained inside her and then slammed back home. Autumn wrapped her legs around his waist.

The bed frame squeaked in protest, but the thing could break for all he cared. He was with his woman, and she would have all of him until she was satisfied.

"You feel so good," he murmured.

Autumn rolled her hips to meet his every stroke until they both raced over the edge. Autumn threw her head back, panting as Jack filled her, stretching and marking her once again.

After a quick shower, Jack insisted that Autumn be examined by the royal tari. Hamilton did as thorough an exam as he could with Autumn fully clothed. Jack nearly needed to be restrained when Hamilton asked her to remove her shirt so he could examine her belly. Autumn had found a purple t-shirt and jeans after her shower and promised to only raise her shirt enough for the tari to see her midsection. Jack sneered at Hamilton the entire time, but Hamilton kept things very professional.

"Princess, you are completely healthy. As far as I can tell you have no ailments or injuries to be healed. However, it does seem like you are very near your transition."

"You think so too?" Autumn asked.

"It makes sense. You are overdue. If I didn't know any better, I would think your powers were bound at some point, but they are emerging now. Maybe this is the cause of some of your accidents." Jack said looking in Matt's direction for a more medical explanation.

"The transition changes your body chemistry, your hormones, and the wiring in your brain. The changes can heighten your emotions. They can also make you more prone to little accidents. Humans don't have powers because their bodies are not strong enough to host them. Our gifts can be pretty volatile. The transition that we go through because of our magical DNA ensures that our bodies don't implode when our full powers emerge," Hamilton explained.

CHAPTER SIXTEEN

"What happens when I fully transition? I mean will it hurt?" Autumn asked.

"No *Kipeyo* it will not hurt. You will only feel exhausted and then sleep for several days. Because of your father's DNA when you wake up, you will be..."

"Like you," Autumn finished his sentence with a glance at Hamilton who stood quietly and did not react.

"Let's go," said Jack. "We need to meet the squad."

Chapter Seventeen

Jack and Autumn joined the kin squad, minus Sage, at Base. Sage was posted outside the queen's bedroom in the mansion.

Jack refused to break contact even now. He held her hand, placed a hand on her thigh, or wrapped an arm around her waist while they sat with the group on the brown leather couch.

"Those were pokeberries in your room. They can easily be mistaken for blueberries if you don't notice the small differences. Basically, you ingested nightshade. It's a miracle you're alive right now. Thank you, Kamara," Carver said.

"You saved me? How?" Autumn asked her friend. How could her friend with zero medical training have saved her life after she was poisoned?

Kamara glanced at Carver and held his gaze for a moment before answering.

CHAPTER SEVENTEEN

"I'm a witch," Kamara declared. "My name is not Kamara Shaw it's Kamara Masina. My father's name is Reece Masina."

A chorus of gasps and expletives filled the room.

Autumn looked to her friend for an explanation, obviously the only one out of the loop.

"My family, the Masinas, helped keep the bakazi royal family safe after their original guard was wiped out by zakari. You are one of a few bakazi still under our protection for one reason or another. My dad asked me to watch over you. He told me you were a wayward and based on your age your transition would be coming soon. Dad knew the binding spell my family used to hide you wouldn't hold, and new magic is like a beacon. He could have tried a stronger spell using the Masina grimoire, but the Opus of Ash has gone missing. He wanted you protected. I'm sorry I couldn't tell you about all this sooner Autumn. You had to find out about your heritage on your own. All I could do was be there to help guide you and keep you safe."

"This is a lot, Kam," Autumn said, shaking her head with wide eyes. "You're a witch? Like a real magic witch?"

"Yeah."

"You know all about the bakazi and my mom? Did you know she was still alive?"

"No Autumn. I swear my dad never told me who you were, only that you were a wayward with no family to help you through the transition."

"Why would you agree to babysit me?"

"At first I was following orders but when I got to know you, I knew you were my sister from another mister. You truly are my best friend. Can forgive me, Autumn?"

Autumn's head was spinning with this new piece of information. Kamara had always been overprotective. As much as she complained, Autumn secretly liked the big sister vibes. And she needed her friend to help her navigate this new life.

"You're forgiven," Autumn responded with a small smile. "Thank you for saving my life." She would have hugged her friend, but Jack had a death grip on her, and she couldn't blame him.

She would probably be a little clingy, too, if she had found him half dead on the floor and then had him magically brought back to life. The thought of losing him made her eyes sting.

"So, you're a Masina witch," Jack said to Kamara. "Do you have any spells or charms to help us figure out who hired an enforcer to target Autumn?"

"Unfortunately, I don't. The stuff I would need is... I can get it," Kam said standing up. "Give me an hour."

"No. You are not leaving this land, Kamara," Carver said firmly before Kam could take more than two steps toward the front door of the barn-dominum.

"Kiss my ass, Carver."

"Bend over, Peaches. I will gladly lay my lips anywhere you like. Especially if it keeps you here and safe."

"Don't fucking call me Peaches you assh—"

CHAPTER SEVENTEEN

"Enough!" Jack's voice thundered through the room. "I'm sorry but Carver is right about this. No one leaves this land for any reason. It's not safe. You could be captured and forced to tell them how to find Autumn, or worse, used as leverage to lure her out. We will find another way. Carver, you were on guard duty in the hall outside the queen's bedroom at the time. You should have been able to see Autumn's door from your post. Did you see anyone go into Autumn's room?" Jack asked.

Carver and Kam were still giving each other battle-ready stares. Carver answered without breaking eye contact.

"I saw a servant go into that room before she got there. A young woman with short brown hair. I've only met her briefly, but I think her name is April."

"April? I know her. I doubt she has a grudge against you, Autumn. Someone had to have ordered her to deliver those berries," Lucky chimed in.

"Why am I not surprised?" Carver asked, finally rolling his eyes toward the ceiling.

"She's a sweet girl. Not a hateful bone in her body. Wants to be a teacher. If she delivered those berries, it was on someone else's orders. The same someone who hired that enforcer demon. Find that person and we find our mastermind."

"You think she'll talk?" Kamara asked. "She's probably loyal to anyone who could have given her that order."

Jack's cell rang before Lucky had a chance to answer.

"What up, Sage? I'm on my way," Jack said before disconnecting the call and turning to Autumn.

"What is it, Jack? What's going on?" she asked.

"Your mother is awake and she's asking for you."

Chapter Eighteen

As soon as they crossed the brown and blue speckled tile in the foyer, Lucky looked at Jack. "I'll go question April and meet y'all back at Base. I'm a little scared Kamara's gonna take a chunk out of Carver if we leave them alone for too long."

"Same," Jack agreed as they reached the second-floor landing.

Jack and Autumn headed to the queen's bedroom while Lucky went to question April. The servants were usually in their rooms by this time of night. Lucky had been to the third-floor bedroom before to visit the young lady. April was a nice girl and a complete submissive. He enjoyed her company very much. He'd only ended things because she deserved better. She deserved someone who could give her a happily ever after. There was no way she was knowingly involved with trying to hurt Autumn, but she might be able to tell him who was.

Lucky knocked on April's bedroom door and waited for an answer that didn't come. He knocked again. Maybe she was already asleep.

"April," he called, hoping to rouse her.

A crash came from the other side of the door.

Lucky turned the knob, but the door was locked tight. He took a couple of steps backward to give himself room. One kick and the door flew open to reveal a shocking scene.

The dowager king, Silas, stared over his shoulder at Lucky's intrusion. He was straddling April's body holding a pillow over her face as she struggled to keep breathing.

"What the hell? Get off her, Silas!" Lucky lunged for the other man, grabbing him by the collar and pulling him free of April.

Silas landed hard on the wood floor.

"It was you, wasn't it? You ordered April to take those berries to Autumn's room."

April sat up on the bed coughing and gasping for air. Her olive skin was now mottled with red and purple. Silas had nearly ended her life.

"I did what had to be done," Silas said with a regal air as he rose to his feet. "And I couldn't risk the maid opening her mouth."

"You son of a bitch," Lucky growled just before his fist connected with Silas's jaw.

Silas stumbled back from the force of the punch.

"April, get out of here. Go to the queen's bedroom. Tell them what happened. I'll make sure this asshole doesn't try to get away," said Lucky.

April eased off the bed on unsteady legs. She kept her eyes on Silas, obviously afraid he would try to somehow finish the job Lucky interrupted.

"It's okay, April. I got you. Go."

April stood still except for the shivers that raked her body. She was in shock. Lucky had to get her out of the room.

"In your current station, you are no more than an attack dog. Kill the maid and I will reward you. Do this for me and you will live like royalty." Silas interjected.

Lucky ignored Silas's awful words and focused on April.

"April. Eyes on me," he said, dropping his voice to a smooth deep tone.

He didn't want to take his eyes off Silas, but it was the only way to get April to safety.

April looked at Lucky. Silent tears ran from her frightened eyes.

"You did so well, and you were very brave, sweetheart. Do you know that?"

"Yes, sir."

"I need you to go to Queen Rayvn's room now."

April moved toward the door while maintaining eye contact with Lucky. She had just passed by him and was nearly over the threshold when Lucky saw a flash of metal. He instinctually pivoted at the same time Silas made his move. The dagger sliced across Lucky's forearm and penetrated his side. April screamed and scrambled down the hallway.

Lucky went down holding his side. He hoped the wound was not deep enough to be lethal. Lucky kicked out just as Silas advanced to no doubt finish him off. Silas fell hard and the dagger skittered across the hardwood floor.

Sage stood in the second-floor hallway guarding the large double doors. A bright smile lit her face and brightened her eyes as Jack and Autumn approached. To most, it would look like a friendly greeting, but Jack knew otherwise. When Sage smiled it meant trouble. She was about to do or say something reckless.

"Sage this is Autumn," Jack said, gesturing to make the introductions.

"Don't you mean *Princess* Autumn? Word travels fast, Jack. It's very nice to meet you. Your mother is waiting," Sage responded, reveling in the gossip about Autumn's birth. She sidestepped to give Autumn and Jack space to push through the double doors and into the queen's bedroom.

Rayvn, who it seemed had been pacing, pulled Autumn into a hug as soon as she entered the room.

"Thank the universe you're okay. The last thing I remember is laying on the floor watching a fireball fly toward you. I couldn't move. I couldn't save you."

"Mom, I'm alright. It's not your fault some demon tried to flambé me."

"Sweetheart, I don't think you are safe here. I came to the cabin to ask Jack to keep you there longer so I could... so I could look into some accusations."

"May I ask my queen what accusations?" said Jack.

Rayvn looked at Autumn with unshed tears in her eyes.

"Sit with me, Autumn," Rayvn said, leading Autumn toward the window seat.

"I have made so many mistakes with you and I am sorry for that. I'm sorry for not putting you first over this damn throne."

"Mom it's okay," Autumn answered softly. "You did what you thought you had to. You tried to keep me safe from the zakari the only way you knew how."

"The zakari are not the only threat to you."

KNOCK! KNOCK!

Sage opened the door without waiting for a response. Her green eyes were back to their usual dark and serious jade.

"I'm sorry to interrupt Your Highness but she says it's urgent."

April rushed into the room on unsteady legs. Swaying a little before reaching out to Sage for a steadying hand.

Sage helped April over to the nearest chair.

"Sit down and speak," Sage ordered.

April's voice cracked as she spoke.

"Your Highness. The royal guard is needed. Lucky is in my room, and he's been hurt."

"What?" asked Sage before giving anyone else time to respond.

"Lucky saved my life. King Silas... he came to my room while I slept and put a pillow over my face. He tried to kill me. He stabbed Lucky in my room. You have to help Lucky."

"Stay here with the queen and princess," Jack ordered.

"No," Rayvn and Autumn answered simultaneously.

"He's my father. I'm going," Rayvn stated.

"Fine but Autumn—"

"I'm not going to let Lucky get killed because of me, Jack."

"Shit!" Jack swore. "We do not have time for this. Lucky could be dying. Sage— Where the hell is Sage?"

"Damnit! Sage!" he called knowing where she was headed.

The queen and princess were not going to back down and without Sage to babysit, those two would follow him anyway.

"Fine. You two stay behind me."

Chapter Nineteen

He could already feel the air shifting as he jogged up the stairs. Someone had started a windstorm on the third-floor. Jack's blond hair whipped all around.

"Watch out!" Lucky yelled. A second later Sage and Lucky literally flew out of the room and into the hall like a clumsy Superman and Wonder Woman then crashed into the other side of the hall in a tangle of arms and legs.

Rayvn and Autumn struggled against the wind to check on them.

"Sage is unconscious but breathing," Autumn said.

"Lucky too but he's bleeding," Rayvn said, pulling up Lucky's shirt to examine the wound. "A nasty gash but not life-threatening."

"We need to move them both out of the line of fire," said Autumn.

Curious servants had opened their doors to see what was happening, fear and shock on the faces of many.

"Cole, come here and help us," the queen asked one of the onlookers.

"Let's move them over by the stairs. They'll be out of any crossfire until they come back around."

"Get back in your rooms! Go!" Jack shouted to the rest of the servants as Cole helped the women move Lucky's and Sage's unconscious bodies out of harm's way.

Things would get messy if the dowager king couldn't be reasoned with. Currently Jack wanted to rip out Silas's throat with his fangs, but he had to be smart. Silas was still bakazi royalty. Killing him would mean death to all involved unless he could prove the dowager king tried to kill his granddaughter. There had to be a community trial. Silas's supporters would accept nothing short of a confession from his own lips which meant he had to be taken alive.

"Silas!" Jack yelled.

"Bring me Autumn West and I will let your friend live."

"Why do you want her?"

Jack moved into the open doorway trying to keep Silas's attention on him instead of Autumn.

"I do not answer to you, orphan. You are nothing more than a walking blasphemy. My Olive was naive to think your kind would protect the bakazi. Your mothers were weak sluts. Their offspring has no choice but to be the same. But you're not weak are you, orphan? You are like your father. A zakari demon who only wants to kill and corrupt, and Autumn West is one of you."

A few days ago, Jack would have agreed. He was like his bastard of a father. He was bloodthirsty and callous. Being with Autumn soothed that part of him. She was his peace.

"You're wrong, Silas. Come with me and we can talk about this."

"She's one of you. She can never lead the bakazi. She should have never been allowed to be brought into this world. I will not let that abomination ruin my legacy. Rayvn will mate again. She can produce another heir, and no one needs to know about that blight she produced the first time. Now bring me Autumn West."

Jack heard shuffling behind him. Someone new joined them in the hall.

"Vervina what are you doing here?" Rayvn asked.

Jack glanced over his shoulder in time to see a female bakazi wrap her arms around Autumn before they both disappeared.

Vervina scattered her cells and took Autumn with her. Jack felt a wave of panic wash over him. Was this person a friend or foe? She had Autumn and could take her anywhere in the world. What if she hurt her? Before he could continue to spiral, they both reappeared inside April's bedroom.

"Thank you, Vervina. I'm so pleased with you," said Silas.

"Thank you, Your Highness," said Vervina

"Dad, don't hurt my daughter," Rayvn said, trying to push her way into the room. Jack held his position.

Vervina reached into her bag and pulled out a syringe filled with silver liquid. She handed it to Silas and turned to Autumn.

"Don't be afraid," said Vervina. "We are not going to hurt you. This will only strip you of your powers. It's a mercury injection. It might cause some temporary unpleasantness, but it passes quickly from what I've seen. Then you can go back to your life just like you were before."

Autumn quickly glanced over her shoulder at Jack and reached for the gold ring on the silver chain around her neck.

"So, if I agree to this shot, I can just walk out of here and back to my regular life? What about that enforcer demon who's after me? Who's gonna tell him I don't have magic powers anymore? Him?" Autumn pointed to Silas. "He tried to have me killed. I don't trust him."

The dowager king placed the syringe full of silver on the nightstand and gripped a dagger in front of his chest blade side down.

"She's an abomination! I will not allow her to carry my family DNA. I would rather bleed every drop out of her."

"She's your grandchild!" Rayvn interjected.

"No. She is nothing to me but a soon-to-be-dead spawn," Silas spat.

"Silas no! Please. That's not what we talked about. No one needs to die." Vervina objected.

"You're weak, Vervina, worse than my Olive. At least she had some dignity. You're just a desperate whore who will do anything I say as long as I ask with my cock up your ass. Now give Autumn to me."

"No. This was a mistake." Vervina took a step backward, taking Autumn with her and away from the dowager king.

"*You* are the mistake. I told her you couldn't be trusted. I asked her to come home and help me rid our kingdom of these obscenities, but she refused."

"Who? Who else are you working with?" Vervina asked.

Jack took his chance to grab Autumn.

Silas refused to let what would be his last chance pass. He launched the dagger at Autumn.

In Jack's mind time slowed down. He saw the dagger sailing toward the woman he loved. He swung her into his position and took hers. Jack waited for the cool steel to push through his spine, but it never did. Instead, he heard a loud gasp behind him.

Rayvn was there, a few inches from where Autumn had been, and her father's dagger was buried in her chest.

"Mikael," Rayvn groaned as she crumpled to the floor.

"Mom!"

The queen had flown in to protect her daughter.

"Mikael if you can hear me. Autumn needs you," Rayvn said quietly with her eyes closed. The queen was sending out a telepathic distress signal.

"What did you do?" said Vervina before scattering her cells and disappearing to no doubt go on the run. She would be dealt with for her part in all this. The squad would track her down and show her firsthand how the silver worked. She had proved she could not be trusted with her powers so they would be taken.

Silas's eyes were peeled wide and trained on the hilt of his dagger protruding from the queen's chest.

"No," Silas said in disbelief.

Black mist appeared in the third-floor bedroom and all hell was truly about to break loose.

"Rayvn!" Mikael yelled racing toward the lifeless body on the floor. As he fell beside Rayvn, he let out the ear-splitting howl of an animal in mortal pain. He cradled her head in his lap and caressed her face.

Silas stood in shock like a statue staring at the dagger sticking out of Rayvn's chest.

"Daughter?" Silas said dumbfounded.

Mikael's head snapped up at the sound of Silas's voice. The room started to shake. No, not just the room, the entire house was moving. Mikael's shattered brown irises glowed. The abnormalities that caused his eyes to resemble shattered glasses traveled down his cheek like tears. Not only did his eyes overflow with hellfire but the intricate white pattern on the side of his face and neck glowed a bright orange as well. The light fixtures in the room began to spark and explode. Mikael hissed and swiped his hand toward the dowager king and Silas floated up to the ceiling. Silas's feet kicked underneath his ever-present dark robes and he started to claw at his neck, desperate for air.

CHAPTER NINETEEN

Mikael clenched his outstretched hand into a loose fist and held Silas in place, enjoying his sickly choking sounds.

Jack threw his body over Autumn to shield her from the chaos. This was a pissed-off full-blood zakari. The temperature of the bedroom began to rise as soon as Mikael spotted Rayvn's bleeding body on the floor. Steam rose from every surface now. Thank the universe the demon was focusing his wrath on Silas and no one else for now. But he would not let Autumn become collateral damage.

"Mom!" Autumn cried.

Mikael's face whipped around to the sound. His shattered irises locked on Autumn and the glowing of his facial markings dimmed until they were white against his brown skin.

The chaos calmed for the moment. Mikael looked down at Rayvn and began to speak.

"Do not give up, Pretty Wings. Remember who you belong to. Body and soul. You will not leave me. I will not permit it."

"Look after our daughter." Rayvn struggled to breathe with every word. "Keep her safe," she coughed. The dagger had most likely punctured a lung. "I love you both," she whispered before closing her eyes.

"No! Mom!" Autumn cried, reaching out for her mother.

Jack wrapped his arms around Autumn giving as much support as he could. She'd lost her mother again.

Mikael closed his eyes and lay Rayvn's head gently on the floor still holding his left hand outstretched toward Silas.

"Get Autumn out of here," Mikael demanded.

Jack stood and gathered Autumn in his arms walking toward the doorway while the flames erupted on the ceiling and the foundation shook again.

When his daughter was safely out of the room, Mikael raised his other fist toward Silas.

"You took what is mine."

Mikael began to lower his fist slowly and Silas let out a hoarse scream as his flesh was ripped open at the top of his head and peeled from his skull. Mikael continued taking pleasure in the screams as the musculature of Silas's lower jaw was exposed. Silas was a snake shedding its skin. Before he could pass out from the pain Mikael jerked his head to the side using his powers to snap Silas's neck and let his limp body fall to the ground.

Mikael knelt next to Rayvn's body and gathered her in his arms before disappearing in a black mist.

Chapter Twenty

Lucky dodged falling picture frames and broken glass on his way back upstairs. Fifteen minutes prior he'd regained consciousness on the third-floor landing. Sage was lying next to him. She looked so small and fragile in her unconscious state. This was the best version of Sage. She couldn't spit venom at him for trying to help her. Lucky scooped her up into his arms and started down the stairs when the building started to tremble. He knew Silas didn't have that kind of power and neither did Jack. Which meant there had to be one hell of a strong supernatural being in the building. None of their enemies would be invited past the blue stone border so this heavy hitter had to be one of the good guys.

Lucky had gotten Sage out of the building as quickly as he could. The newcomer might be a friend but the havoc they were wrecking did not seem to discriminate. Once outside he walked another thirty feet before laying Sage in the grass. It had nothing to do with him enjoying the feel of her in his arms. He wanted to make sure she was a safe distance away from the mansion in case it all came tumbling down.

After making sure Sage was safe and somewhat comfortable Lucky jogged back to the mansion and up the stairs. Three staff members ran past him screaming and holding their forearms above their heads for protection. Chunks of the ceiling were breaking loose and making things even more dangerous.

"Go! Get outside!" came a shout from above.

Jack cradled Autumn in his arms and hurried down the stairs.

"Is it clear up there?"

"Yeah. Staff's clear. We gotta go," said Jack.

By the time the group made it to the brown and blue speckled tile of the foyer, the shaking had stopped but there was an acrid smell of smoke in the air.

Jack sat Autumn on her feet. She was visibly shaking. Jack held her close, rubbing a hand up and down her back in an attempt to calm her.

"What the hell happened up there?" Lucky asked.

"Mikael. My father. He's gonna kill Silas," said Autumn in a shaky voice.

"Silas lost his fucking mind. After he knocked out you and Sage, he started yelling for me to give him Autumn." Jack pulled Autumn closer to his body and continued. "No way I was letting that happen but the next thing I know Autumn is in the room."

"How?"

"Vervina was helping him. She thought Silas would inject Autumn with the silver and that would be it, but Silas just wanted her dead. Queen Rayvn flew in just as Silas made his move and... she didn't make it."

"No. Are you saying she's gone?"

Jack nodded his head.

"We need to keep everyone calm," Jack said.

The staff all sat close together on the front lawn trying to comfort each other. April waved to him while talking to the house chef.

Lucky looked toward the spot where he'd left Sage on the grass. She was alert but holding her head as if she was in pain. They had both gotten thrown like rags and woken up to chaos.

A tall older man walked over.

Smoke rose from the top of the roof now.

"The fire department is on its way. I grabbed my phone on the way out," he said.

"Thank you, Cole. And thanks for helping out up there," Jack replied.

"Of course, sir," Cole answered before leaving to rejoin the staff.

Jack took Autumn's hand in his and started to move toward Base. She had been through so much tonight and was obviously in shock. He needed to take her somewhere quiet and comfortable to lay her down and keep her warm until she came out of it.

"Come on baby. We're going to my room. You need to lay down."

"She was trying to protect me," Autumn whimpered.

"She loved you. This is not your fault, *Kipeyo*."

Autumn started to tremble so much that she almost seemed to vibrate. Then her eyes flashed a bright amber.

"My mother is dead," came her thready reply.

Those were Autumn's last words before her body went slack against Jack.

"Autumn. Fuck! She's transitioning," said Jack.

Autumn woke up to the sound of someone talking.

"This isn't funny, Dean. The voice says I'm almost..."

"Out of minutes," she said along with the angel from her favorite TV show.

"Autumn," Jack's voice interrupted one of her favorite shows on television.

"Thank the universe you're awake."

"What happened?" she asked.

"What do you remember?"

"I remember you carrying me out of the mansion with Lucky behind us. We were standing on the front lawn and then... I don't remember anything. How did I get here?"

Autumn glanced around the room not even sure where *here* was. The room was dim, but she could see that all the furniture was oversized. The bed was a regular king sized but she seemed to be more than three feet off the ground. Made for someone with legs much longer than her own. Either she had discovered the land of giants, or this was Jack's bedroom.

"The stress of... everything that happened triggered your transition. You've been out for two days," Jack said.

Autumn sat up on the bed, eyes round and one hand over her mouth in shock.

"Why does my mouth feel weird?" she asked.

"Your gums are probably a little sore from your new fangs."

Autumn explored her mouth with her finger, pricking herself when she found the evidence she was looking for. The taste of her own blood was no longer a copper tang. It tasted more like salted caramel on her tongue.

Autumn swung her feet over the side of the bed. She was wearing one of Jack's T-shirts again and the oversize shirt crept up revealing Autumn's bare bottom as she slid off the extra-high bed frame. Jack reached out to lend a steadying hand but his gorgeous blue eyes wandered down to her exposed flesh. Autumn made no move to cover herself. She felt no shame with Jack and as she made her way to the dresser the soft cotton t-shirt righted itself.

The reflection in the dresser mirror was surprising. It was her face but different. Her skin looked smooth and glowed like it was illuminated from the inside. Her eyes had lightened to the same amber shade as her father's and her lips seemed fuller, too, though that may have been due to the addition of her brand-new fangs. Autumn lifted her upper lip to get a better look at her new K9s. She was officially a magical creature. She was a spawn. A freakin' fanged bakazi demon.

Her curls were as unruly as ever but now had red highlights like her mom's.

"My mom?"

"I'm sorry, baby. When we went back into the mansion the queen was gone."

Autumn met his eyes in the mirror.

"Will you help me plan her funeral? I don't know anything about bakazi burial customs or traditions."

"If you want to have a ceremony, I will help you plan it but Autumn, we never recovered your mother's body. When I say she was gone I mean she was missing. We think Mikael may have taken her."

"What? Are you sure? I mean I think they loved each other for however long they were together but why would he want to take her body with him? That's just weird. Where would he even go with her? Maybe her body was destroyed in the fire."

"The fire was contained to the ceiling. We think Mikael used it to torture and kill Silas. But I have to admit taking the queen's body is a strange thing to do, even for a zakari."

Jack wrapped his arms around her.

"I am so sorry, *Kipeyo*," he said, dropping a kiss on the top of her head.

She'd nearly been killed by her grandfather and his mistress.

Thanks to Jack and the rest of the kin squad Autumn was still on the right side of the dirt. He was her protector. It was hard to believe they had known each other for so little time. Meeting Jack had changed her entire life. Well, that wasn't exactly true. Learning about her heritage had changed her life but Jack was the one who dropped the truth bomb. She had gotten to spend time with her mother. Her best friend turned out to be magical and in a broken relationship with a spawn. But she knew their situation would work itself out.

Now Autumn had a group of people she considered family. A village. She knew they would look out for her, and she would do her best to look out for them.

She was still coming to grips with the fact that she was not only a bakazi, but part zakari, too.

"Vervina. Did you find her?"

"Not yet but the kin squad will not stop until we do and I will put that silver injection in her arm myself. Of course, he would. He was her protector.

"And we can try to find your mother, *Kipeyo.*"

"Do you think Mikeal found a way to heal her?" Autumn asked.

"Almost anything is possible with magic."

Autumn was searching for closure. After her mom drowned, Autumn simply accepted the news. She was a child. The police said her mom's body must have been swept away. But obviously that had not been the truth. She needed to be sure this time. What if her mom was alive somewhere and trying to get back to her?

Autumn turned in his arms to return his embrace. It felt so good to have him wrapped around her. Safe and quiet.

"I love you."

"And I love you, Autumn West. My partner, my mate, my princess."

Autumn smiled, wrapping her arms around his neck to pull him in for a kiss.

Jack deepened their kiss and slid his hands down her curves, pressing himself even closer to her. She moaned into his kiss and pressed her chest against his.

Jack gripped her thighs and lifted her to sit on the dresser. Autumn had to spread her legs until they were nearly flat against the hardwood surface to accommodate his size. The position turned her on even more.

"Are you feeling alright? The transition can be draining."

"I want to be close to you," said Autumn.

She nuzzled against his naked chest for a second before pulling him in for another kiss. This time she grazed his bottom lip with her new fangs and reached for Jack's pants.

"Thank the universe for an elastic waistband. Easy access," she said.

Just a little tug and her prize sprang free. She would never get tired of the feel of him in her hands. Soft and hard at the same time. At this moment, she needed to forget the world and get caught up in her own love story. She rubbed his penis against

The End

EPILOGUE

"Father?" She looked him in the eyes. Autumn needed Mikael to understand that no matter how he claimed to feel about her mother he had abandoned them. He was a stranger to her.

"Never had one. You got Mom pregnant and then poofed out of her life. She was scared and on her own. She had to leave her home to keep me safe. Where was your desire to be a father then?"

Mikael held her gaze and gave a slight nod.

"Okay. We may not have a relationship, but I will be watching over you. I will make sure your ascension is not challenged."

"Ascension?"

"To the throne."

Autumn took a step backward and shook her head.

"I don't want the throne. Look what it did to my mother. That fucking throne has ruined my life."

"It's what your mother wants. It's your birthright and she thinks you have the compassion and backbone it will take to lead the bakazi. For what it's worth, I agree."

"She *thinks*?" Autumn raised an eyebrow. "Why are you talking about her in the present tense like she's still alive?"

Mikael's eyes darted to the trees.

"Our time is up. I have to go, Autumn. Take your place as queen. Your mother will not return."

Epilogue

The warm breeze felt good on Autumn's face while she watched the treetops dance at her feet. The beautiful wood bridge she stood on twisted and curved above the canopy of lush green. She walked along the winding path, reaching out to touch the green leaves.

"Is this heaven?" she said.

"Hello, Autumn."

"Mikael?" Autumn turned in a slow circle, taking in the picturesque landscape. "This can't be hell."

"No. This is someplace else. It's breathtaking, isn't it?"

"Where am I and what is happening?"

"You're sleeping and this is Africa. Well, a version of it, anyway. I brought you here so we could talk. I wish things could be different for you little one, but I want you to know I will never regret being your father."

CHAPTER TWENTY

her thigh savoring the intimacy. As she started to stroke him Jack growled.

"Enough *Kipeyo*."

"You never let me explore," Autumn pouted.

"We have a lifetime for you to play. Remember I belong to you, and you belong to me." Jack took himself in hand and pushed into her. Autumn wrapped her legs around him, urging him as deep into her as he could.

"Why do you still call me *Kipeyo*? You've touched every part of me."

"And I will never stop touching this gorgeous body. But you are better left untouched by another unless he wants to lose whichever part touched my beautiful butterfly."

Autumn smiled up at Jack as he started to move inside her. His overprotective nature was unnecessary but sexy as hell because she felt the same way about him.

Jack was right, they would have a lifetime together because he belonged to her, and she belonged to him.

Content Warning

This book contains the following content that may be difficult for some readers:
- Adult Language
- Biting
- Choking
- Graphic Violence
- Nudity
- Sexual Assault

Made in the USA
Middletown, DE
17 May 2024